Sherlock Holmes
and the
Three Poisoned Pawns

Emanuel E. Garcia
Roger Jaynes
Eddie Maguire

Edited by Antony J. Richards

A Sherlock Holmes murder mystery anthology
First published in 2008
under the Breese Books imprint by
The Irregular Special Press
for Baker Street Studios Ltd
Endeavour House
170 Woodland Road, Sawston
Cambridge CB22 3DX, UK

© Baker Street Studios Ltd, 2008

ISBN: 1-901091-29-5 (10 digit)
ISBN: 978-1-901091-29-8 (13 digit)

Cover Concept: Antony J. Richards

Cover Illustration: From a specially commissioned watercolour by Nikki Sims
featuring Highcliffe House with insets of Hamlet, Lord Salisbury and the Kaiser as
the three poisoned pawns.

Typeset in 8/11/20pt Palatino

Contents

Sherlock Holmes
and the
Mystery of *Hamlet*

Emanuel E. Garcia

About the Author

Emanuel E. Garcia has published numerous articles on the history, practice and application of psychoanalysis, which include investigations of the composers Mahler, Rachmaninoff, Delius and Scriabin. As an offshoot of his psychotherapeutic work with classical musicians he introduced a method of practice designed to enhance the performance of string players which appeared in the *American String Teachers Journal*, on whose editorial board he serves.

A native of Philadelphia, he currently practices psychiatry in New Zealand and continues his work with creative artists, lecturing to students and the faculty at the New Zealand School of Music and members of the New Zealand Symphony Orchestra.

The works of Edward de Vere, P. G. Wodehouse and Sir Arthur Conan Doyle have been perennial sources of joy.

Foreword

Upon his death my uncle Sir John H. Watson entrusted to me, as executor, his literary estate. He generously gave me *carte blanche*, asking only that I exercise 'common sense' when it came to publishing the cases and notes that were archived in Cox and Co. bank at Charing Cross. As a result, accounts of the Sumatran rat, the red leech, Wilson the canary-trainer, the story of the lighthouse, the affair of the aluminium crutch, the steamship *Friesland*, etc., were eventually incorporated into a complete standardised edition of the Holmes' chronicles. The world has, I believe, been the richer.

The present manuscript, that I discovered serendipitously within a cache of yet to be catalogued miscellanea, bears several marks of distinction. First, for reasons as yet to be ascertained, it was neither complete nor filed away with Sir John's other meticulously preserved case reports at Cox's Bank. Second, the action of the tale – if action it can be called that – occurs in the last year of Holmes' life, and both its principal content and evidence of Sir John's visit are corroborated by Sigmund Freud in the only extant allusion to the chronicle: an as yet unpublished letter addressed to my uncle and dated 23rd May 1939. Finally, it is a singular example of the application of Holmes' science of deduction to literature and as such reveals a striking and novel facet of the great detective's powers.

I am certain Sir John would never have wished t withhold an account of his friend's most unique triumph from the general public.

James J. Watson, Esq.
London

Saturday, 16th July 1938

It has been over a decade since last we met. I had travelled from London at Holmes' unexpected and urgent request – his summonses were always urgent – and I wondered what new game might be afoot, unlikely as it might seem given our advanced years. Europe was on the brink of cataclysm. Could it be that as before my dear friend had been engaged by a representative of the Government to match wits against an increasingly dangerous and evil foe? As I strolled along the gravel path leading to the door of his cottage in Sussex, I could not help but admire the quiet natural beauty of the surroundings in which the great man had chosen to spend the days since his retirement from criminology.

On my right lay an extensive herb garden whose curiously mingled scents recalled for me the markets of Afghanistan, and to my left in the distance ranged hive upon hive of the apiary to which Holmes was now devoting so much of his intellectual acumen. Surprisingly enough I could hear from the direction of his cottage the harmoniously plaintive sounds of violin and piano borne aloft by a gentle afternoon breeze.

Had Holmes arranged for a celebration of our reunion? If

so, it would be most unusual. Nonetheless the mere thought stirred me deeply. Though my ear was not a particularly musical one – not at all up to the fine standard of my friend's – the strangely exquisite harmonies and the tender yet strong melodic lines fit so unerringly into the Sussex countryside that I found myself rooted to the spot, quite overcome by emotion. Fearing to disturb the spell being woven by this strange compelling music I lingered motionless on the path until the final notes had died away and the low insistent hum of bird and insect life re-assumed prominence.

As I approached the threshold the door swung open before I could knock and there stood my dear companion, virtually unchanged save for his now silvery-white hair, as fit and lean as he had been at Baker Street. His incessantly observant grey eyes were sparkling.

"Watson!" exclaimed Holmes as we warmly clasped hands. "Time has treated you well I see."

"Holmes!" I stammered, scarcely able to pronounce his name as my eyes brimmed.

"Come along, my dear fellow," he continued, "and allow me to introduce you to someone."

I coughed and brushed my cheeks with the sleeve of my overcoat. Not since Holmes' miraculous reappearance in my rooms years after I had believed him to be dead had I experienced such emotional consternation. Luckily this time I did not faint – had I done so, I would have been deprived of an exquisite sight. Just under a window that overlooked a lovely patch of verdant terrain was a piano, and sitting at the instrument was an extraordinarily handsome young woman.

"Mrs Grant, this is the dear comrade-in-arms of whom I have so often spoken," announced Holmes. By now I had fully – no, *thank*-fully – regained my composure.

She rose courteously and I took her hand in greeting. A sweet pang reminded me of my long-deceased wife Mary. There was something so familiar …

"Well, Watson, do you see the resemblance?" interrupted Holmes.

I gazed intently at her enchanting countenance. Years of intimate association with the most acutely perceptive mind in Europe had not gone wasted.

"Could it be, Mrs Grant," I tentatively inquired at last, "that you are related to our former landlady, one Mrs Hudson?"

She smiled broadly and Holmes nearly leapt wit excitement.

"Watson, you exceed my expectations!" he cried. "I see that my methods have left a legacy. Fancy that here in my retirement from the fog and crowds of London I should yet encounter a reminder of the old days. As you undoubtedly have already ascertained, Mrs Grant is an accomplished pianist, and as a vicar's wife she has ample occasion to exercise her musical artistry for her parishioners' benefit."

"But where is her partner, Holmes? I distinctly heard a violin and, meaning no disrespect to Mrs Grant, she was every bit an equal."

Holmes grinned.

"*She*, Watson?"

"Well, such delicacy of touch could only be attained by a feminine nature – it was the stamp of a virtuoso; and judging from the splendid interplay with Mrs Grant, it must be someone with whom she practices assiduously." I grew heady with conjecture. "A sister – yes! Mrs Grant, I believe you have been accompanying your sister – an elder sister, I should add – and that her absence now can mean only that she has excused herself to powder her nose in preparation for imminent departure."

I must say, I fully expected Mrs Grant's elder sister to appear momentarily. Holmes was shaking his head and Mrs Grant blushed.

"Watson, Watson, I am afraid I spoke too soon," said Holmes, nearly convulsed with laughter. "You should have stopped after your early triumph of detection. Mrs Grant is indeed related to our dear landlady – she is her grandniece – *touché!* But her musical partner stands before you."

I was astonished. Naturally I knew of Holmes' penchant for picking up the fiddle and scraping away for hours on end in Baker Street, particularly when involved in a case that tested his intellectual prowess. But today I had heard an artist – not an amateur – of the instrument.

"If you'll excuse me, Dr Watson, but I really must be returning to the vicarage," said the captivating Mrs Grant, adding mischievously while taking her leave of Holmes, "my sister awaits."

I seated myself, flustered and flabbergasted, and Holmes brought out the cigars.

"Watson, bee keeping and horticulture have been daytime pursuits – my nights have not been idle. Music has much occupied me. Did I not send you my treatise on the polyphonic motets of Lassus?"

"Yes, Holmes, of course – but your musicological research would not suffice to explain this new found virtuosity at a time of life when one's physical powers cannot but have deteriorated significantly."

"Watson, you are much too much a follower of so-called 'scientific' prejudice. We improve with age, my dear man – with age the wealth of our knowledge and experience, the complexity of our understanding – they enhance our powers! Too many of us are lulled by superstitions into neglecting the cultivation of mind and body. My hair may be white, Watson, but I can assure you that the organ it protects is keener than ever! And you would be amazed to learn what a creative mind may attain, even under the most inauspicious conditions."

Holmes beamed with enthusiasm.

"The music you heard moments ago, Watson – would you believe that it was composed by a man blind and paralysed, a man in nearly constant pain who required the unstinting assistance of others to do what you and I take for granted? Would you believe that a man in such a state would be able somehow to convey musical ideas of such exquisite and complex beauty to an amanuensis?"

"Impossible, Holmes, impossible!" I retorted.

"No, my dear Watson, not impossible, but fact. Implausible, perhaps, but true. Had you spent less time in the billiard room the names Fenby and Delius might be familiar."

I bristled under Holmes' condescension.

"However, to return to your questioning of my musical technique ... I have always maintained, Watson, that if a fellow merely takes the time to observe he will inevitably discover something of value. You will admit my fondness for the violin, and I will admit my extraordinary good luck in securing for myself at so little cost an instrument of such merit as the Stradivarius. Unfortunately during the salad days of our criminal investigations I had neither the time nor enthusiasm for the refinement of technique to do this magnificent instrument justice. But here in Sussex, among my bees and plants, I have been blessed with both."

Holmes poured two brandies and fetched two more cigars.

"In my concert-going excursions I always paid particular attention to the solo violin, and I noted invariably that the wheat and chaff among soloists could quite easily be separated. The truly outstanding violinist, Watson, would be capable of playing *pianissimo* – but with a most robust and accurate tone; furthermore, he – or she – could also play both *presto* and *pianissimo* simultaneously. Lesser musicians can play fast only if they play rather loud, and are generally unable to project a rich sound in passages requiring utmost sensitivity."

As a physician I now warmed to the topic.

"It seems to me to be a matter of fine muscular control, Holmes: lesser control invariably involves compensatory pressure – in other words, one disguises one's deficiencies by pressing with greater force upon the strings."

"Precisely, Watson. Reasoning thus, I thereupon devised a very simple but quite effective method of practice which resulted in the virtuosic display – if you will pardon my immodesty – that graced your ear today."

"Holmes, I cannot help but admire you! How did you do it, what were the particulars?"

"They were – elementary, my dear Watson!"

Holmes and I both laughed at the deliberate misquotation from my chronicles, which had made its way into common parlance.

"I wilfully abandoned all inclination to produce a beautiful sound and concentrated instead on playing extremely slowly and softly – painfully slowly and softly, Watson, painfully ... It was anguish at first, I can tell you – but gradually, over the ensuing weeks and months I discovered that I could produce twice the tone with half the effort – and much more accurately than ever – when I played up to speed and volume. I need not bore you with every detail, but I am especially proud of the fact that the series of exercises I devised included, at appropriate stages, the purposeful elimination of *vibrato*, and also a deliberate restriction of the lateral movement of the bow to a narrow channel strictly parallel to bridge and fingerboard. Suffice it to say that I have never played better. Miracle, Watson? No, mere common-sense – with a dash of discipline."

"Holmes, you leave me speechless," I answered.

"A paradoxical response if I've ever heard one," he retorted wittily.

"But here, let me demonstrate."

He ran to snatch his fiddle and proceeded to illustrate the methodology, stage by stage. As a medical doctor concerned with physiology I was captivated by the obvious efficacy of these simple but masterful technical exercises, and as a friend I marvelled.

"I hope I have made my point, Watson," continued Holmes as he replaced the violin in its case, "and I also hope that you realise something of the valuable psychological consequences of practicing in this manner."

Holmes paused, peering strangely at me.

"I have not yet been able to publish these findings because a matter far more pressing has absorbed my attention of late."

A feverish glow had suffused Holmes' face, so familiar to me from the past during periods of acute excitation preceding the *denouement* of an especially challenging case. I confess, however, that I wondered about the darker side of my friend's personality. The consternation must have been apparent, for Holmes' air grew perceptibly lighter and his words reassuring.

"You need not concern yourself with my health, Watson. I

have grown far too sensible, and I am no longer dependent on the thrill of the chase for sustenance. No, my pursuits have been rich and engrossing. I fear the golden age of criminal detection has disappeared, and a new one is upon us. Today the great criminals are criminals of state: artless, transparent and brutal. Even the Lestrades of the world are losing ground, their services confined to petty and guileless infractions. I see a time in the not too distant future – if there is a future, that is – when the gathering and correlation of evidence will be completely mechanised, and the Moriarties of society will exhaust their stratagems no longer as members of the underworld but as legitimate politicians! No, Watson, we have had our day ..."

Holmes mused, blowing desultory smoke rings towards the ceiling.

"I do not mean to say that the principles upon which I exercised my faculties are obsolete or invalid – only that their fields of action have been altered. My studies in horticulture and bee keeping, in music and even in literature – yes, Watson, you thoroughly underestimated my love of letters – have been immensely satisfying."

"Tell me, Holmes, of your discoveries – surely you have retained the capacity to astonish."

Holmes smiled. He was a softer, graver man this evening.

"The wonders of nature, Watson, and the wonders of mankind at its best – in its exercise of the creative imagination in both art and science – they are limitlessly rewarding. You might say that my former obsession with the darkest, most devious and destructive aspects of human existence was a kind of preparatory schooling for my present preoccupations, of which you unfortunately know so little. Our most exhausting adventures are as nothing compared to the rigours of my recent investigations."

I sat entranced by the quiet enthusiasm of my friend who teased me with the promise of other mysteries.

"Take bees, for example, Watson. Mere insects – of interest to our species primarily for the honey they produce. Would it surprise you to learn that these fascinating organisms can speak?" Holmes asked impishly.

"Preposterous!" I involuntarily exclaimed.

"I did not say 'talk', my friend – no. But bees have indeed evolved a language of no little specificity and sophistication."

"Go on, Holmes, " I replied.

"During the years preceding the Altamont affair I had occasion to correspond with an Austrian entomologist who at my suggestion pursued a line of research leading to the discovery that bees can perceive colour – and more. They can signal to each other the exact location of food sources – by dancing."

"The next thing you will have me believe is that they can sing too," I expostulated.

Holmes laughed kindly.

"Well, they do buzz – you will not deny that, will you? But they also dance. If one of their scouts discovers a source of food close to the hive – say, a particularly fragrant cluster of flowers rich in nectar – upon his return he executes what my correspondent von Frisch calls a 'round dance' which marshals the inhabitants of the hive to fly forth to their treasure. But there is more to it, Watson. I believe I have finally persuaded von Frisch to my view that there is yet another kind of dance, a dance that is distinctly different – it involves waggling."

"Waggling?" I interjected, mildly stupefied.

"Yes, it is a 'waggle dance', my dear fellow." Here Holmes

traced what looked to be figure-of-eights rapidly in the air with his forefinger. "The 'waggle dance' is employed to signal the location of food sources at a considerable distance from the hive, beyond 50 meters. Amazingly enough the particulars of the dance indicate quite precisely both the distance of the food source from the hive *and* its direction in relation to the position of the sun. In short, Watson, bees have their own language – and a most remarkably articulate one. As I have often told you, when the impossible is eliminated, whatever remains, no matter how improbable, must be the truth."

I merely shook my head.

"Like you, von Frisch was incredulous at the suggestion, but I have no doubt that my facts will win him over."

Holmes indicated volume upon volume filled with the meticulous observations he had charted over the years. He continued.

"As another Austrian friend of mine – rather *ours* I should say – is fond of asserting, 'the voice of the intellect may be soft, but it inevitably gains a hearing'."

"Professor Freud?" I queried.

"Who else? Have you heard, Watson, that he is now in Hampstead, safely removed from Vienna? His health, I am afraid to say, is poor, but his mind is as acute as ever. Not even the Nazis could diminish his droll wit."

We sat in silence for some moments, enveloped by thoughts of the nightmare that was threatening to consume all of Europe and perhaps even the world.

"They will destroy themselves, Watson," said Holmes, as if telepathically following my reflections, "but not I fear before they destroy many others."

Holmes sank into a reverie, oblivious of me and of his surroundings, his face by turns sad and fierce in the light of the glow from his nearly spent cigar.

"Yet," he exclaimed abruptly, "I have forgotten the peas!"

I was utterly confused.

"Peas? Have they been left on the stove unchecked" I asked naively.

Holmes coughed and spluttered in mirth and it took some time before he could calm himself.

"No, no, no, Watson, have you ever known me to cook so much as an egg? The peas I am referring to are peas that I have been growing."

"Holmes, I'm afraid I don't follow: to what purpose would you grow a vegetable if not to eat it?"

"Watson, my dear man, have another drink," he continued genially, also proffering a fresh cigar. "Cuban, Watson, they are without equal."

I nodded appreciatively.

"Let me explain. Yet another Austrian, now deceased, demonstrated through the cultivation of pea plants, certain laws of inheritance. He published his findings in 1866 in a brilliant paper, *Experiments in Plant Hybridisation* – a paper that was virtually ignored for decades. They are breathtaking, Watson, for what they imply about heredity, *if*, that is, his observations are truthful. He was, by the way, a monk, and therefore possessed both means and time to conduct his research, as I do now in abundance. I am still attempting to replicate his experiments, Watson, and although I am convinced that in the main monk Mendel is indeed correct, I have consistently observed complexities that cannot lend themselves to his oversimplifications: the results are too clean, Watson ... Something a bit rotten, perhaps, in the state of Denmark."

I was wholly at a loss and could muster merely an

inarticulate grunt in response.

"Which brings me, my dear friend, to the matter for which I summoned you."

Once again an impassioned gleam animated Holmes' angular face, and then an angelic voice called from the recesses of the cottage.

"Mr Holmes, your table is ready – and I hope I have cooked the peas to your liking."

Mrs Grant was every bit a culinary artist as a musical one, and the table she set provided amply for the feast of reason and flow of soul. My confusion and anxious desire to know more of Holmes' secret were mitigated by the exquisitely prepared meal and the discussion it catalysed. Holmes and I exchanged summaries of our last decade, mine engaged in compiling additional chronicles of our exploits, as well as venturing into the domain of historical fiction, his in the numerous researches to which he had already alluded. Neither of us could be said to have developed any friendships that approached the intimacy and strength of our indelible partnership.

From time to time Mrs Grant, who sat with us, joined in to tell of her interests. I found my eye drawn to that lovely animated face, and on the occasions when she turned my way I confess to have blushed.

Nonetheless her attentions were drawn primarily by Holmes whose features, even in his eighties, remained sharp and attractive. His was not a conventionally handsome face, but it radiated intelligence and drive. Had he been forty years younger and she unmarried I would have assumed that he and Mrs Grant were affianced, but I knew full well that Holmes' energies did not lie in the direction of romance: he was constitutionally incapable.

By and by Holmes held forth and captivated us both with tales of the secrets of bees and plants and, astonishingly enough, investigations into the *belles lettres*, and even psychology. He had kept up a lively correspondence with Professor Freud of Vienna over the years, and his opinions were sought after by some of the most eminent university men in England, though he held them in low esteem.

"Academia is to knowledge as Scotland Yard is to criminal detection!" he exclaimed, as we pushed away our chairs and repaired to his study.

Except for the absence of bullet marks on the wall, it was nearly identical to the Baker Street flat in design: our armchairs were similarly positioned in relation to each other and to the fireplace. I felt younger and lighter as my heart raced in anticipation of Holmes' imminent revelations. He lit his pipe and I took yet another cigar. The evening summer air was cool.

"Watson," said Holmes gravely, "your services as a chronicler have been immense, though I have disagreed with your tendency towards dramatisation, nonetheless you have successfully captured the essence of my methodology in criminal detection."

He fixed his eyes upon me.

"What would you say, dear friend, if I were to tell you that my wildest successes pale in comparison to what I have recently achieved? What would you say if I told you that I have solved the most profound and puzzling mystery in all of literature?"

I studied Holmes closely. My medical training fought with my kinship as Holmes' friend: had he succumbed to the delusions so typically attendant upon the advance of old age?

"You must think me mad, Watson, perhaps because I

intimate that I value more the solution of a literary conundrum than that of a murder?"

"Holmes, you do not do my friendship justice," I remonstrated.

"This is not a matter of friendship. You will base your judgement on whether my achievement has merit solely on the facts I present, dear Watson."

"Naturally, Holmes, just as before."

"My inquiry was instigated by a most unlikely source. Ten years ago, Professor Freud had requested my opinion on an historical thesis that could not be dealt with adequately by post. I hastened to Vienna and, having arrived early at his office, amused myself by initiating a conversation with a gentleman's gentleman waiting for his employer, a genial but vacant youth, who was just then consulting the doctor. The man was perusing *Spinoza* and our conversation led to matters of morality and the unfortunate tendency of the ruling classes to mistake privilege for accomplishment. He cited one of the more egregious exemplars of such kind and he described the effect he elicited from others rather vividly, quoting a phrase from Shakespeare's *Hamlet*. I discerned at once that he had derived the quotation from the *First Folio*, which I held to be inferior to that of the *Second Quarto*, and I divulged this opinion. After a lively discussion of Shakespearean publication, this extraordinary man brought to my attention an aspect of the play that had entirely escaped me hitherto. I was seized on the spot by a visceral emotion, for I sensed, Watson, that he had touched upon something of tremendous import – so much so that I could not help but apprise Professor Freud of the conundrum that very evening. Freud was astonished, and it was to him that I owe the impetus for pursuing the matter as vigorously as I had pursued Moriarty."

I grew sad, recognising at once what my friend would now assert. Though determined to remain calm – to humour him to prevent further embarrassment – I could not suppress my genuine sentiments.

"For heaven's sake, Holmes, don't tell me that you dispute the authorship of Shakespeare. I cannot bear to see your brilliance so tainted by such folly."

Holmes tilted his head back and a thin coil of smoke issued from his pursed lips. He exhaled very slowly.

"Watson, your stubborn conventionality is almo charming. I do not hold it against you – this belief that an illiterate from Stratford-upon-Avon authored the greatest works in the history of literature. Sadly we have all of us been reared in this preposterous myth."

I frowned.

"But Holmes ..."

"No, Watson," retorted Holmes sharply, "how many times must I advise you to look at the facts?"

He continued with some vehemence, leaning forward for emphasis.

"There is not one of them, not one piece of incontrovertible evidence to link the Stratfordian bumpkin to the plays of Shakespeare, not one, Watson. Although the question of authorship is peripheral to the matter for which I requested your presence, it is not wholly to be ignored. You have brought your travelling bag with you, I trust?"

I nodded.

"Good. Then let us spend what remains of the night in going over facts – or the lack thereof, Watson. We will have ample time tomorrow, my friend, for the crux."

I knew it would be no good to protest, eager as I was to

dismiss with preliminaries. Holmes had quite obviously retained his exasperating ways, and though he often chided me for over-dramatising his adventures it was really he who was the architect and stage-manager of surprises. I recalled as if it were yesterday seeing his shocking silhouette against the bleak night terrain of Dartmoor and discovering later that Holmes had taken residence on that forbidding and desolate wasteland while I had been sending my painstaking dispatches to our address in Baker Street.

"Where do I begin, Watson? I will make it rather simple. In fact, allow me to be so presumptuous as to borrow an approach from a friend of mine (who, incidentally, may play a critical role on the stage of world history in the coming years): let us conduct a 'thought-experiment'."

My curiosity was piqued.

"Is it not true, Watson, that you have achieved some small renown for your literary efforts?"

I conceded as much.

"Why yes, Holmes, I suppose that my efforts have reached an audience of sorts."

"You are far too modest, my friend. Thanks to you our names are on the lips of every London schoolboy, not to mention that bastion of bureaucratic mediocrity otherwise known as Scotland Yard. And you, as author of the chronicles, have been mentioned even among the most exclusive of literary societies. I speak of Bloomsbury, naturally."

I managed a genial smile. It was true that I had received more than a modicum of acclaim for the style and skill with which I rendered my accounts of Holmes' genius, and it was also true that I feared Holmes would misunderstand this as a deviation from my chief aim, which had always been to present to the public at large his magnificent wisdom. Indeed, many times I had deliberately downplayed my own role in our criminal investigations so as to throw Holmes' accomplishments into greater relief.

"Now, Watson," continued Holmes, "on the occasion of your inevitable death – which I hope will not occur before my own, for purely selfish reasons – would you anticipate a public reaction – tut now, my dear man, do not be so self-effacing."

"Well, Holmes, to be frank, I am certain it would warrant a notice in *The Strand* and very probably *The Times* as well ..."

"At the very least, my friend, the very least. Your obituary would in all likelihood be known throughout Europe, and for years to come a stream of literary obeisance and praise would pour forth, not to mention special commemorative reissues of your works and quite probably the posthumous publication of your notes. You would undoubtedly inspire others to take up the pen and invent *new* episodes out of whole cloth. Do you not concede truth in this, Watson?"

I smiled and glowed beyond my usual modest restraints.

"Your funeral – not to be overly morbid, my dear fellow – would be attended by a multitude, including heads of state, especially if my information is correct about your impending knighthood ..."

My heart leapt. I knew my friend had refused the offer, but for myself such a thing, was ardently, if secretly, hoped for. I had not Holmes' insouciant disregard of public honour.

"And if I were so unfortunate as not to have preceded you, I would be among them, mourning deeply."

I was touched to the quick, and speechless at his uncharacteristic display of emotion.

"Now then," continued Holmes, collecting himself, "would you not also concede that, notable as your literary achievements may be, they pale somewhat in comparison, say, to fellow countrymen such as Keats or Shelley or Byron or Milton?"

"Naturally, Holmes." I laughed heartily: even to be mentioned in the same breath as these giants was absurd.

"And in comparison to the person whom the known world regards as the greatest of literary geniuses ..."

"Holmes, my dear fellow, what are you driving at?" I found myself growing inexplicably testy.

"Would you then find it curious, Watson," replied Holmes, ignoring my interruption, "that the death of this greatest of authors would go without remark at the time?"

I stammered in an attempt to grapple with the question.

"Not a word, Watson, not a word. The death of Shakspere – yes, that is the correct name – of Stratford warranted no mention whatsoever. That the man regarded as the flower of his age, the man who moved royal and common audiences alike, enlarged the language in an unprecedented manner, the man whose works – *pace* our Viennese professor – are the greatest psychological testament to the soul of the race – that this man, Watson, should pass away and not arouse a single comment even in the town of his birth ..."

Here Holmes paused, feverish and sharp as of old when in the hunt.

"Is it not highly suspicious, to say the least?"

I confessed; indeed, I had never considered the matter before.

"Good, Watson: it shows that you have still an open mind. Let us proceed. Before your hypothetical death, you will no doubt have left a testament."

"I have already done so, Holmes."

"Naturally. And in that testament, as a man of letters,

might I hazard the guess that you have made arrangements for the disposition of your library?"

"Yes, in fact ..."

"No need for details, Watson, the point suffices. You regard your books as property of value; they have been dear friends throughout your life and you wish to bequeath them to the deserving."

"I cannot argue with you there, Holmes."

"Now, Watson, it might interest you to know that the fellow from Stratford, in his own last will and testament, being particularly concerned about household furniture and other trivia, makes no mention whatsoever of anything literary: not a book, not one single book, not a play, not a poem – nothing of the kind, absolutely nothing."

I was discomfited and remained silent.

"A very palpable point, no?" teased my friend. I was unable to respond.

"And now," he continued, "for our last little thought-experiment. As a successful man of letters, Watson, you have conducted quite a correspondence, I should imagine."

"Why yes, Holmes – all very carefully preserved, I might add. For quite some time now I have followed Cicero's example and retained copies of what I have written to others."

"Excellent. But consider: should the letters in your possession be inadvertently destroyed or discarded or stolen, one might expect your correspondents – at least *one* of them – to have retained a few of your missives."

"At the very least, Holmes."

"Very good! However in the case of Shakspere, not only does no letter from his hand survive, but no letter from any of those to whom he must undoubtedly have written survives either: not a single one. Considering the enormous regard in which the author of the plays and poems attributed to Shakespeare was and has been held, does this not raise a question?"

"Holmes, you have raised more than a question; my head is spinning with conjecture."

"Let it spin a little, Watson, and while it spins let me sum up the results of our experiment. The greatest literary genius in human history dies, and no contemporaneous mention of his passing is made. No letter from his hand has ever been found, nor has any letter *to* him ever been brought to light. Finally, in the last testament of this most literate of men there is no mention whatsoever of anything literary."

"Like the curious incident of the dog in the night-time," I shouted.

"Precisely, Watson – the dog that did not bark."

Holmes glowed with satisfaction while I sat in a daze. In a matter of minutes he had deftly penetrated a cherished illusion which, though disturbing, had me once again marvelling at the man's abilities.

"But if not the Stratfordian, then who?" I queried.

"Oh, that question has already been answered," replied Holmes casually, "by an intelligent man who just so happens to have a most unfortunate name. I played some little part in the investigations that led to the discovery of the true author of the Shakespearean canon. Just after the Great War, Watson, I was approached by a schoolteacher – a modest fellow, thoroughly steeped in the works of the Bard, whose sensibility simply refused to countenance the Stratfordian mythology. He inquired how one might go about conducting a rational and systematic inquiry into the question of authorship, and after giving the matter some thought, I suggested a methodological approach which he subsequently employed and which led to the precise identification of the man behind the works. *Shake-Speare* is, incidentally, a fairly obvious *nom de plume*. Looney – spelled L-O-O-N-E-Y – don't laugh, Watson, it is unbecoming – published his discovery in 1920 – I am surprised you are not familiar with *Shakespeare Identified* – and though I differ from the gentleman in certain assertions (his discussion of *The Tempest*, for example, is not a fruitful one), I am wholly in agreement that Edward de Vere, the seventeenth Earl of Oxford, was the creator of *Hamlet* and the entire *oeuvre* attributed to Shakespeare. Looney's work has, by the way, thoroughly convinced our friend Dr Freud – no small achievement, mind you ... But I fear that our time is growing short. Great as this matter may be, it is beside the point. This is not the mystery for which I summoned you."

"Holmes, I am immensely curious – what mystery can be greater?"

"I said to you earlier, Watson, that I was devoting attention to *literary* detection – not biographical. In the long run does it matter who the man was, or what name he bore, so long as his words continue to enchant. No, the greater mystery concerns the greatest of his masterpieces, the greatest drama to engage us, a work which, if all others were to disappear, could alone suffice to rebuild the language and art of the theatre." Holmes paused and brooded. My fingers were nearly burnt by the stub of my neglected cigar as I waited tensely.

"*Hamlet*," whispered Holmes, "I have solved the mystery of *Hamlet*, and in so doing I have unmasked the most treacherous villain in all of literature – the foulest, basest, and, I confess, smoothest monster, a character to which Moriarty would be negligible, against whom Iago or Macbeth are as children in evil."

29

"For heaven's sake, Holmes, who was it?" I implored.

"Tomorrow, Watson, tomorrow. The night is late."

I was incredulous.

"But Holmes!"

"Be patient, Watson. Before I say a word more I wish to ask a favour."

"Anything in my power, Holmes, anything," I replied with fervour.

"Watson, you have always been far my superior with the pen, a far better chronicler of my own deeds than I. I care little now for those youthful exploits – but I regard this literary excursion as the chief accomplishment of my life: and if I succeed in convincing you, my dear friend, I wish you to record it for posterity."

"Holmes, it will be an honour," I said with warm candour.

"You will perhaps not think so after tomorrow – but I wish you to promise."

"I promise, Holmes."

"Again, Watson," cried Holmes sharply.

"I promise, dear friend, you have my word," I replied, taken aback by Holmes' excited insistence.

"Good," said Holmes, settling. "Now, let me show you to your room."

Sunday, 17ᵗʰ July 1938

I slept fitfully, restlessly, disturbed by unremembered dreams and awakened by what I imagined to be a muffled caterwaul. Leaping briskly to my feet and hastily donning a robe I staggered out of my room towards the sound, only to find Holmes in his dressing gown, working away at the fiddle.

"Good morning, Watson!" said Holmes cheerily. "Breakfast will soon be served; but before you retreat, listen to this."

Holmes played the *Meditation from Thais* with a richness and beauty that charmed me out of any disgruntled state.

"I am attempting to master Sarasate's *Caprice Basque,* but I fear that age does have its limits, which no method can overcome. So be it, Watson, we must allow the young some scope … Mrs Grant will have our victuals ready in half an hour – the day beckons and I trust your appetite is as keen as mine."

Mrs Grant was even more enchanting in the morning … My eyes involuntarily lit on her every dance-like movement and I breakfasted as if in reverie. Holmes absented himself, promising to return shortly, and I took the opportunity to stroll outside the cottage. That curious aroma which had recalled the days of my youth beckoned, and as I cursorily inspected the numerous plants and flowers I spied beyond the herb garden a fair-sized greenhouse. I began to make my way towards it when Holmes, with a speed that belied his age, fairly ran me down and I felt his iron grip about my arm. I thought for a moment that I saw alarm in his grey eyes as he guided me back towards the apiary on the other side of the cottage.

"I must tend to my flock, Watson, before anything else can be done. Here, put this on."

Holmes handed me a mask to cover my face and neck but he himself went without one. He moved briskly and fluidly from hive to hive and the bees seemed to form a respectful arc above his head. It was all I could do to keep from flailing away wildly as they buzzed about me, but Holmes remained serene and intent. When finished he took my arm – this time quite gently – and proposed a walk.

"The better for me to form my thoughts, Watson. This road leads to the coast. Let us go and I will explain all."

At last! The day was cool and I was brimful of anticipation. Holmes lit his pipe and offered me a cigar. It would prove to be the most extraordinary walk of my life.

"Watson," began Holmes, "do you believe in ghosts?"

"You know me better than that, Holmes."

"So you say, so you say – and yet if I recall correctly, the legend of a certain supernatural hound once preyed upon your imagination for a while, did it not?"

"Given the circumstances ..." I began to reply, but Holmes interrupted.

"Yes, given the circumstances the most rational of men will

doubt their reason and accept as utterly probable the grossest of superstitions – under the *right* conditions. Why only recently a man of great public standing, renowned for sobriety of ratiocination, has come forth publicly to profess a belief in faeries – faeries, Watson!"

Holmes puffed, pensive.

"Prince Hamlet believed in ghosts, did he not Watson?"

"He believed in one ghost, Holmes, so far as I know, the ghost of his father."

"But *was* he, Watson – was what Hamlet saw really the ghost of his father?"

"It was a literary device, Holmes, something to set the action of the play."

"So they say, Watson. And so the greatest play in the history of our language, *any* language, begins with something utterly and absurdly ridiculous – a ghost."

"Holmes – if memory serves me correctly, it would not be the only time. In *Macbeth* there is Banquo's ghost ..."

"Yes, Watson, you are correct, and your point leads to an important observation. But in *Macbeth* Banquo's ghost is a representation of the protagonist's inner mind – a projection of his guilt, if you will. Only Macbeth *sees* it, by the way. But throughout the first act of *Hamlet* the case is quite different." Holmes paused.

"Literature is complex, Watson, generally more complex than the life it represents and ennobles: bear with me. I submit to you that the spectre Hamlet saw at the outset of the play was most decidedly *not* a ghost, simply because not only Hamlet but Bernardo, Marcellus and Horatio also saw the figure. It *appears* but once more during the play – in Act III, when Hamlet is alone with his mother. Because it is neither heard nor seen by Gertrude, we may thus unequivocally regard the phenomenon as a dramatic representation of Hamlet's psyche: a hallucination – his brain's *coinage* as the Queen says. However, the figure of Hamlet's father that sets the wheels of the play in motion – this figure is *not* a ghost, nor did Shakespeare mean him to be understood as one."

I was taken aback.

"If not a ghost, Holmes, then what was it?"

"That, my dear friend, is the mystery which I have solved, and in solving have exposed a most unsuspected villain. Watson, the Bard has fooled us for centuries. But the answer has been right before our eyes: he has been teasing us, Watson. I can hardly describe the immense satisfaction it has been to match wits, even posthumously, against a mind so great. I promise you, Watson, that you will never be able to regard the play as before, and that a new dimension of human depravity, an even greater depth to this greatest of literary works, will be vouchsafed to you."

I remained silent, perplexed. Holmes was *on form*.

"One word – one *slip of the tongue* as Professor Freud would say – holds the key."

The air was brisk. I wondered what spectacle we two old men presented to an observer, smoke curling upwards over our closely inclined heads and slightly stooped shoulders as we tramped towards the sea.

"Have you reread *Hamlet* or seen it enacted recently, Watson?" Holmes asked.

"It has been many years, I am afraid ..."

"A pity, Watson, but I will refresh your memory. I have lived with the play, its every word, for some time now. It is a marvel, a miracle of creation, impossible of course to summarise. Line after line of the drama has entered our language. And of what does it treat? Of nearly everything,

Watson: it is a world unto itself. Fathers and sons, wives and lovers, brother and brother, sister and brother, mother and son, man and woman, friend and friend, friend and foe ... It treats of politics and the State, of love, of lust, of warfare, of murder and intrigue. It ends as a veritable charnel house of slaughtered bodies. Nothing and no one are as they seem, Watson – and this is the key. The drama is, above everything, about deception and betrayal."

Holmes paused and I saw his face in shadow: a *frisson* of pain had swept through its features momentarily before he continued.

"Hamlet's father is betrayed by his brother Claudius, as is Hamlet himself of course. Gertrude has unwittingly – so we think, at least – betrayed her husband. Claudius betrays Gertrude in conspiring against her son the Prince. Ophelia is betrayed by Hamlet, and Hamlet by Ophelia, Laertes and Polonius, not to mention Rosencrantz and Guildenstern. Laertes is betrayed by Polonius, his own father, who sends an emissary to spy on him in France. Fortinbras may even be said to have been betrayed by his uncle, who at Claudius' request seeks to rein him in. And *in fine* it is the state of Denmark that is wholly betrayed. Is there anyone who does not betray or is not betrayed?"

Holmes paused again, as if to gather strength for a further thrust.

"So now we must ask ourselves the same question even the most pedestrian Inspector of Scotland Yard asks at the outset of any investigation: *cui bono*? And the answer is quite obvious: Fortinbras. The young warrior has annexed an entire country without so much as spilling a drop of his soldiers' blood. And what a sense of timing. Does it not strike you as more than coincidental that Fortinbras should enter the court of Denmark precisely at the time of its demise? Was it luck, Watson, pure chance? No, my friend, Fortinbras was aided in his enterprise: he employed a *mole* – a term which my brother Mycroft has informed me is now common in British Intelligence."

"You mean a spy of sorts, Holmes?"

"More than a spy, Watson, but a hypocrite of the first order – someone who labours in the guise of a helpmeet to the person or agency against which he deviously sets his sights. Can you follow, my friend?"

A light mist hovered over the ocean as we emerged from the road and faced the vast impenetrable sea, and as we stood, contemplative and speechless at nature's reminder of human frailty, the fog within my own mind began to lift.

"Holmes," I shouted, breathless, "it cannot be – but – are you saying?" I stammered incomprehensibly, as my companion looked coolly askance.

"Who else, Watson?"

"But he is the one beacon of honesty, the one true friend, the one representative of the virtue of fidelity – indeed, aside perhaps from Hamlet himself, the one noble, if relatively uninteresting, man within the entire play."

"So he has seemed, Watson, and so it has appeared for all these years. Oh, the Bard has been mocking us – until now, that is."

I was quite overcome, for although I dimly perceived the unsettling truth of what Holmes was intimating, I could hardly comprehend the particulars: it made no sense. As if on cue the sea-air grew chill as a mass of heavy clouds rolled in and the crash of wave against rock intensified.

"Imagine, Watson," cried Holmes, turning and sweeping his arm towards the sea, "imagine Elsinore at midnight and the 'dreadful summit of the cliff that beetles o'er his base into the sea', a half-crazed grief-ridden Prince beside himself, lured and goaded by the most consummate of villains – a master actor and psychologist. Oh, the irony is precious, Watson: it is Hamlet's philosophy that is wanting, that cannot dream of such perfidy in its heaven and earth. And how must his 'friend' have smirked to hear those chiding words. Yes, Watson, it was Horatio."

I was stricken, stunned, unable to distinguish the roar of the ocean from the roar within my teeming brain.

We turned slowly and in silence began to make our way back to the cottage heedless of the falling rain. Holmes brooded serenely as I struggled to grasp the impact of his thesis. Horatio was a minor and incidental character, Hamlet's beloved sidekick, as it were, someone remembered for unwavering friendship, but whose mind lacked depth, someone to whom at play's end Hamlet would nevertheless entrust the sacred mission of reporting his cause aright.

Though the rain grew heavy we could see a patch of blue in the far sky telling us that the showers would be brief – typical Channel weather. Happily a welcoming fire in the cottage's sitting room greeted us, along with a kettle of piping-hot tea and local bread garnished with Holmes' harvest of honey. My friend resumed his discourse without preliminaries.

"The Bard left the perceptive reader a clue, Watson – in retrospect, a glaring one – the *slip* to which I earlier referred. In the very first act, the *ghost* of Hamlet's father, which has already appeared twice before to the soldiers Bernardo and Marcellus, makes another entrance and this time Horatio is with them: he has accompanied their watch on the battlements of Elsinore. Marcellus asks Horatio if the spectre resembles the late King, and Horatio replies in the affirmative:

> 'As thou art to thyself. Such was the very armour he had on when he th'ambitious Norway combated. So frowned he once when in an angry parle he smote the sledded Polacks on the ice.'

He gives the impression, Watson, of being rather familiar with the deceased King, does he not?"

"Why yes, Holmes."

"Yet, Watson, in the very next scene, this same Horatio, called upon to bear witness to his friend the Prince, tells Hamlet that he has seen his father but once: 'I saw him once. He was a goodly king.' I saw him once," Holmes repeated for emphasis. "If this is true, if Horatio had only seen the King but once, why did he say otherwise beforehand and why would Marcellus have looked to him for confirmation of the ghost's resemblance? Is there not at the very least a contradiction, Watson?"

"I cannot dispute this, Holmes," I replied.

"How then are we to rectify these two contradictory statements – in any meaningful way, I mean. One may, I suppose, react like one of our illustrious literary academicians, who asserts that it is simply a waste of time trying to make sense of Horatio's utterances and who sees the character purely as a *factotum* or *dramatic device* doing whatever the so-called plot requires. The immortal Bard doesn't create characters, he creates literary devices. Ah, the pleasures of academe – where all thought is disbarred. I presume you to be capable of a more informed response – to be puzzled by this contradiction and at the very least to be provoked into looking more closely at everything else Horatio says and does."

"I agree wholeheartedly, Holmes – indeed, I chafe to peruse the drama at the earliest possible opportunity for precisely that purpose."

"Good fellow. I submit to you, Watson, that we must conclude that Horatio is a liar."

I nodded in reluctant obeisance to the fact.

"Now then, as you and I know from our investigations, criminals unwittingly reveal themselves – they leave evidence of the crime, Watson, not deliberately of course, but quite unconsciously, either because they are forced into ineptitude by circumstance or because a sliver of conscience betrays them. Horatio has quite fleetingly but quite unmistakably exposed his dishonesty. Thus in one fell stroke, Watson, Shakespeare casts a cloud of suspicion over him, a suspicion that demands a minute and comprehensive examination of the entirety of his actions and utterances. This, as you shall see, will lead to a far more satisfying and coherent interpretation and, taken in conjunction with the weight of other evidence, paints a portrait of manipulative evil that is peerless. It allows us also to solve other problems, not least of which is the rank absurdity that a man has risen from the dead – the 'undiscovered country from whose bourne no traveller returns' as Hamlet quite rightly states (and, as an aside, the Prince's slip indicates that deep within his bosom he knows, Watson, that his father was never resurrected). Do you follow me?"

"I am following, Holmes," I answered breathlessly.

"Ah, Watson, this is why I require your talented aid … I hardly know where or how to begin to address and describe these problems short of compiling an inventory word by word and line by line. The task is to illustrate them clearly to an audience. For this I must rely on your literary skill, for I know that just as in your many accounts of our criminal cases, you will create a luminous and convincing narrative. Not that I advise you to indulge your own penchant for the theatrical, my dear fellow. But I have no doubt you will be able to present the facts to the public in a way that will render them most interesting, cogent and impossible to disavow."

"You honour me, Holmes, and I can promise you my very best effort."

"I shall need it, Watson, I shall need your very best. Are you ready for a smoke?"

Holmes rose and began to pace the room; physical activity always seemed to enhance his cogitations.

"Watson," said Holmes, "I must proceed in a rather unusual way, departing from my customary manner to meet the exigencies of literary detection. Rather than delineate the painstaking and perhaps tedious exegesis informing my discovery, I will instead alight on several salient points. You will have ample time to corroborate them later with chapter and verse.

"One must first entertain the notion, based on the evidence revealed by his slip of the tongue, that Horatio is *not* what he seems. Once one decides to accept, quite hypothetically even, that Horatio is a suspect in the fall of the house of Denmark, then the many disregarded inconsistencies associated with his presence loom with coherent significance.

"Let me enumerate a few. First, Horatio is not generally thought to possess an especially broad or astute mind. And yet his analysis of Ophelia's madness reveals him to have been a master psychologist – listen, Watson:

'Her speech is nothing; Yet the unshaped use of it doth move the hearers to collection. They aim at it, and botch the words up fit to their own thoughts, which, as her winks and nods and gestures yield them, indeed would make one think there might be thought, though nothing sure, yet much unhappily.'

What Professor Freud calls the *mechanism of projection* has been most beautifully anticipated and elucidated. And Horatio remarkably addresses the emotional core – what Freud would call 'Affekt' – of her utterance: sadness. While others are interpreting her ravings according to their own whims, fancies or needs, Horatio has penetrated to the quick. Remarkable, no?

"Second, the timing of his arrival at Elsinore. Does it not strike you as odd that Horatio claims to have arrived for the funeral of King Hamlet? Even the most parsimonious calculation of the time elapsed between the King's death and Gertrude's marriage to Claudius would make him a most unpunctual mourner. Furthermore, his arrival coincides nearly identically with the appearance of the King's *ghost*.

"Third, his behaviour as a friend ... Is it not surprising that though he is at Hamlet's side during the Prince's most fraught moments, he never attempts to protect his ostensible friend by physically detaining him from danger – from running off for a *tête-à-tête* with the *ghost* or from making his way towards the fatal duel with Laertes. He gives lip service, Watson, nothing more. In fact, it is Horatio who ensures that Hamlet can be alone with the *ghost* and even detains Marcellus from following to guard his Prince.

"Finally, not only does Horatio survive the carnage at the

Danish court, but he emerges, with rather sudden force, as a budding orator – a Lord Chamberlain in the making. Again, Watson, *cui bono?* – Fortinbras *and* Horatio.

"Now then, would you not agree that these points raise suspicion, Watson?"

"Yes, Holmes, they raise suspicion, but that is hardly ..."

Holmes hastily interrupted.

"That is all I ask of you, Watson, to accept that these observations, in conjunction with Horatio's blatant dishonesty, raise suspicion. Horatio had the guileless trust of his friend Hamlet, and the psychological astuteness, to do to him what Guildenstern attempted to do – to play upon him:

> 'Why look you now, how unworthy a thing you make of me. You would play upon me, you would seem to know my stops, you would pluck out the heart of my mystery, you would sound me from my lowest note to the top of my compass; and there is much music, excellent voice in this little organ, yet cannot you make it speak. 'Sblood, do you think that I am easier to be played on than a pipe? Call me what instrument you will, though you can fret me, you cannot play upon me.'

"So rails Hamlet against the traitorous Guildenstern, little knowing that his other schoolmate, to all appearances the soul of fidelity, is both fretting and playing upon him mercilessly.

"On the basis of such suspicion, and upon an exceptionally close reading of every word, every nuance of the play, I wish to present a scenario – an interpretation, to be more precise."

Holmes paused to refill his pipe, then settled himself into

his armchair. He was calm and level as he addressed me with gravity.

"Now then, Watson, let us consider the political situation of Denmark when the drama begins. Claudius, the brother to the late King, is on the throne and Denmark is on a war footing. There is 'daily cast of brazen cannon' and 'such impress of shipwrights, whose sore task does not divide the Sunday from the week' and makes 'the night joint-labourer with the day'. And why? As Horatio – most interestingly enough – informs us, Denmark is girding itself for a possible attack by Norway. The late King Hamlet, 'pricked on by a most emulate pride', had been challenged to single combat by King Fortinbras of Norway, whom he vanquished – and in so slaying won the Crown lands of Norway – those lands in which the King served as tenant-in-chief and which were private sources of revenue that could be disposed according to his fancy. The 'sealed compact' preceding this kingly duel specified that Hamlet, had he lost, would have forfeited his own lands to Norway. Young Fortinbras, the heir to the throne of Norway, suffered by his father's death in being bereft of a considerable part of his inheritance. Had King Hamlet been slain, then our Prince would have been similarly impoverished.

"Young Fortinbras, understandably in dudgeon, has amassed an army of sorts and, as Horatio tells us, seeks to recover the lands his father lost. Although it is hardly likely that the young man could successfully challenge Denmark, Claudius is taking no chances.

"Let us pause for a moment, Watson, to consider the implications of the duel. A duel between Kings in which territories of state are wagered is at the very least foolhardy and rash – for either party. A responsible monarch would not

– like either the elder Fortinbras, who apparently goaded his adversary, or the elder Hamlet, who had not the suave patience to pursue diplomacy – have participated in such an enterprise. One may justifiably conclude that King Hamlet, though perhaps a formidable warrior, was not so reliable a governing monarch. Imagine, Watson, risking one's country's lands on the fate of hand-to-hand combat. 'Impulsive and megalomaniacal' is how Professor Freud characterises the action – signs of 'profound pathological narcissism' – perhaps a harbinger of senility.

"In any case, the King's younger brother, who could see beyond this 'victory' must have been shaken and appalled by his elder's behaviour. To preserve the state, his beloved country, he killed him quietly – in such a way so as not to plunge Denmark into turmoil. It was very cleverly done, Watson. That he was so readily embraced as monarch, that Queen Gertrude so easily accepted him as husband, and that the populace showed no signs of unrest – these speak volumes. The only disgruntled subject is apparently young Hamlet."

"But Holmes," I interjected, "was not Claudius motivated primarily by lust for the Queen?"

"Lust, Watson, or love? Surely King Hamlet, an irascible and impatient man, who appears to have relished every opportunity to show his prowess in combat, was not the most reliable of spouses. And just as surely lust could not have been the overarching motive for his brother: Claudius would have had ample opportunity to gratify his lusts as a powerful member of the Court. He loved Gertrude, and it must have pained him to see her treated so irresponsibly and carelessly by his brother. But far more importantly, Watson, did it pain him to witness the recklessness with which King Hamlet jeopardised his homeland.

"I submit to you, Watson, that the murder of King Hamlet was above all else an affair of state, and that we have every evidence that Claudius, a far more sober man, bent all his energies upon securing the safety of Denmark and her subjects. For example, rather than risk his countrymen's lives by initiating a retaliatory action against Norway in response to young Fortinbras' provocations, he resorts to diplomacy while simultaneously strengthening Denmark's military preparedness – he pursues the peaceful means of appealing to Fortinbras' uncle to rein in the upstart.

"Young Fortinbras has no chance against the might of a well-prepared state like Denmark. Indeed, he must have rued the death of King Hamlet: no doubt he would have relished issuing another challenge which the King could not in his pride refuse. And with youth and the fires of revenge on his side, Fortinbras would have stood an excellent chance of achieving his ends. Claudius of course could never be seduced into such folly.

"No, Watson, Fortinbras and his band of 'lawless resolutes' would have to pursue a more effective strategy – indeed, the *only* effective strategy possible: to destabilise the very court of Denmark. *To destroy it from within* ...

"As you know, Watson, I do not believe it is a coincidence that our knowledge of the young Fortinbras' actions comes almost entirely from Horatio – which means of course that we must view it sceptically. True, Fortinbras has amassed a band of followers, and later in the play he and his army are granted safe passage through Denmark to contest a worthless plot of land garrisoned by the Poles. Horatio, Watson, is using a red herring to pull the denizens of Denmark off the true scent: Fortinbras' small group of soldiers on their own are no real threat. No – but Fortinbras needs a martial force at hand for the time when Denmark's court crumbles."

Here Holmes sighed, and I could see that the complexity of his task required a tremendous amount of sheer mental concentration.

"Horatio ... Well, Watson, whether Fortinbras, through a delicately devious stratagem enticed him, or whether Horatio, for motives I will more freely speculate upon later, first offered his services to the enemy of Denmark – you can see that I lean towards the latter explanation – cannot be ascertained. But once we consider the idea that Horatio is the instigator of all that befalls Hamlet and the state of Denmark, then all falls into place.

"Imagine a brilliant but impoverished youth – Horatio, I mean – schoolfellow of a spoiled Prince (that 'observed of all observers'), even perhaps an intimate at Wittenberg where they studied together, allowing Horatio an appreciation of the many facets of his loquacious royal companion's personality ... Imagine this Horatio, chafing like Richard III at the injustice of birth that elevated one of lesser talent above him, or more simply consumed like Cassius by pure envy, or like Iago by jealousy, given that his undeserving companion had earned the love of the beautiful Ophelia who, like Horatio, would forever be beneath the Prince's station ... Imagine this man hatching a psychological stratagem of such sophisticated simplicity and ruthless efficacy.

"Yes, Watson, it was all so relatively simple. Destabilise Denmark by persuading the Prince that Claudius has committed regicide, and thus set into motion a process that would become unstoppably destructive. Consider, Watson – if Hamlet had acted immediately and struck down Claudius, he would have been hard put to survive. Most likely he would have been considered a traitor to the throne and executed for high treason. How could he have justified the deed, what could he offer as proof of Claudius' guilt – a ghost's word vouchsafed only to him? The succession to the throne would have been in tatters, ripe for the plucking, and Fortinbras, loitering nearby with his cadre of ruffians and perhaps the galvanised soldiery of Norway, would have been able to press his advantage. Even if by some miracle Hamlet had persuaded the populace of the justice of his cause, Fortinbras would have leapt at the chance to throw his weight against one who, though an admirable courtier, had hitherto evinced no talent for governing.

"Horatio's task was an infernally simple one – to catalyse chaos – but to do so irrefutably and cogently and then, at the appropriate time, to signal for Fortinbras' *coup d'etat*. Hence a ghost ...

"Horatio – like others at the time – may have suspected Claudius of foul-play ... Indeed, I believe that his psychological acumen convinced him of its plausibility. As it turns out, of course, Claudius admits to fratricide – for his crown, his ambition and his queen, as he confesses to himself in a moment of weakness at prayer, personal guilt overriding responsibilities of State – and this coincidence is favourable to Fortinbras' and Horatio's aspirations. But it was completely immaterial whether Claudius had actually murdered his brother the King: it was important *only to convince Hamlet that he had done so*. Once the cantankerous, moody, violent and wily Prince had been let loose to trouble Claudius, it would merely be a matter of time, and of the timing of Fortinbras' thrust.

"But how could Horatio effectively sew doubts in Hamlet's breast — doubts sufficient to set the landslide in motion?

Horatio would have courted incarceration or death for treason had he openly suggested something so blasphemous as regicide. No, my friend, that was far too dangerous a route to take – it could never have been hazarded. Nor would he have been assured of its carrying any persuasive weight. But a father's ghost – here is a different matter altogether. I cannot but marvel at the beauty of it Watson – it was the only way, the only way."

"But Holmes," I interjected, "how do you account for the figure itself, the apparition? Surely it could not have been Horatio in disguise."

"Assuredly not, Watson. It was obviously someone in his employ: someone dearly in need of money, and someone furthermore capable of …"

I could not help myself: I burst out, leaping to my feet and scattering ash all round me.

"Of acting, Holmes – it was an actor!" I exclaimed.

"Precisely, Watson. You do yourself credit."

Holmes smiled and knocked the ash out of his pipe neatly into a receptacle.

"If you recall, Watson, the arrival of the dramatic players in Act II – the troupe that will perform the play wherein Hamlet seeks to 'catch the conscience of the king' – the very fact of their travelling, rather than maintaining residence in the city, indicates the hard times they have fallen upon. As Rosencrantz informs Hamlet, child actors have become all the rage and their elders ousted from the lists, as it were. Thus the occasion for seasoned players to visit Elsinore. It would not, therefore, have been difficult for Horatio to entice one of their number, destitute as they were, to impersonate the ghost of King Hamlet – to have clothed and bedecked him in the appurtenances of the late King and given him his lines. Oh, there was true genius, Watson. If you remember what a little luminescent phosphorus spread over the jowls of a dog achieved on Dartmoor, it is not so hard to imagine that a passable disguise, to men already tense in the wee hours, would be harrowingly convincing. Why, I dare say I have occasionally deceived you, Watson, with my impersonations."

I chuckled and nodded in agreement.

"Without doubt, Holmes."

"Listen carefully, Watson – you will have to reacquaint yourself with the Shakespearean text much more comprehensively later – but the game is afoot. Horatio employs an actor – perhaps the same player who so convincingly recites the tale of Priam's murder at the hands of Pyrrhus – and instructs him to appear silently on the ramparts of Elsinore 'in the dead waste and middle of the night'. The already shaken guards are thrown into consternation. Meanwhile Horatio just happens to have arrived at Elsinore himself, and as the known friend and schoolfellow of the Prince (his only friend so far as one can tell) he would have been the logical choice for the guards to corroborate their frightening vision.

"Horatio feigns disbelief and must be entreated to confront the apparition: he knows well not to overplay his hand. So he 'reluctantly' agrees to accompany the watch. On that night the ghost appears – silently – then disappears, and the guards look to Horatio the scholar to address it. When it reappears Horatio charges it to speak, but it recedes silently again. What tension, Watson, what drama! Horatio has scripted it marvellously. And not only can he write, but he can act: he seems to tremble and turn pale and makes sure no one doubts that it is indeed the late King. The ghost appears yet again – for the third time that night – and Horatio musters the courage to challenge it more forcefully, to demonstrate all the more conclusively its presence and identity. He has also arranged for its exit to conform to accepted superstitions – when the cock crows the dead must return to their 'confine' – about which Horatio is all too glad to explain to the others. For verisimilitude he instructs Marcellus to apprehend the ghost and even to strike at it with his spear – quite confident that the terrified Marcellus, 'distill'd Almost to jelly with the act of fear' the night before, would be as accurate as you were in your attempts to fend off the bees earlier today. It was a most impressive piece of theatrical subterfuge, Watson.

"But Horatio's task is hardly over: it remains for him now to engage the Prince. He must do so convincingly and definitively. When once engaged, Hamlet would do the rest. As intimately as he may have known the Prince and as astute a psychologist he may have been, I doubt whether even Horatio could have predicted the exact shape of the relentless unfolding of events: but he must have foreseen what powerful turmoil the Prince was capable of instigating. It remained for him merely to bide his time, to be vigilant, and to keep Fortinbras – waiting in the wings – informed.

"We all know, of course the bloody tragedy that ensued. But I outpace myself ..."

Holmes' momentum, however, was unstoppable. He barely took time for breath before continuing.

"The most delicate part of Horatio's mission is yet to come. Once Bernardo and Marcellus have seen the vision and he has confirmed it, it is time to approach the Prince. Horatio does so with witnesses in tow – an essential and wise move.

"Now for another incongruity. When Horatio greets the Prince it is clear that Hamlet had been unaware of Horatio's arrival at Elsinore until just then. He at first seems not to recognise him, then inquires why he has travelled from Wittenberg.

"So the question arises, Watson – why hasn't Horatio presented himself to the court beforehand, when he first arrived? Of course you and I now know the answer to that – he has been busying himself with preparations for treasons, stratagems and spoils."

I nodded. Holmes' case was growing stronger by the minute. My scepticism was diminishing exponentially as the evidence accrued. How could so many inexplicable events, so many incongruities have been so overlooked for so long?

"Then, Watson, at their re-acquaintance," continued Holmes, apparently pleased with my demeanour, "Horatio stokes the fires of Hamlet's troubled psyche – a bold move, Watson, one he would need to make as a way of promoting an acceptance of the ghost's message to come. Listen to the exchange:

> 'Horatio: My lord, I came to see your father's funeral.
> Hamlet: I pray thee do not mock me, fellow-student; I think it was to see my mother's wedding.
> Horatio: Indeed, my lord, it followed hard upon.'

Horatio then proceeds to tell the Prince of the ghost and he is at pains to vouch for its identity with his father. And he slips yet again, Watson. In his enthusiasm to convince Hamlet that his actual father had arisen from the dead, he says 'I knew your father; these hands are not more like'.

"Can you believe it, Watson? Just a moment before he had

told the Prince that he had seen the late King but once – *once*. And now he declares an intimacy with him that the alarmed Prince cannot even think to call into question.

"Horatio has stirred Hamlet and goes on to embellish, describing the ghost's countenance as sorrowful and pale. Well, Watson, all the better for a ghost to be pale – for a player's greasepaint to be luminous and obscuring at night. He is then so bold – driven of course by his game – to warrant that the ghost will reappear to Hamlet.

"The Prince takes the bait – he agrees to accompany the next watch."

Here Holmes unexpectedly paused and rose.

"Watson," he asked quietly, "do I bore you?"

"Why no, Holmes," I protested.

"Good, my friend, for I fear that the matter is quite complex and I strain to be clear. You will have every chance to check the text in your leisure, to assimilate the facts and lend your sturdy judgement."

"Holmes, I am keen to do so, but I can tell you that your case is both fascinating and strong. I am already convinced."

"Not yet, Watson – do not be so rash. Hear me out and then you may confirm or otherwise dismiss my findings quite easily. In some ways now, Watson, it is all rather anticlimactic. The great coincidence of the play is that Horatio has hit upon the truth – that Claudius *has* killed his brother – which works to his immense advantage. The principal task, as I have said however, is to convince Hamlet to seek revenge and either to topple Claudius or be toppled himself. In either case the distress in Denmark's court would leave an opening for Fortinbras.

"The ghost's appearance to Hamlet was the crowning glory of Horatio's perfidious talents: what a consummate dramatist, Watson, what a persuader. I need not review each pregnant line of the ghost's scripted utterances, but merely to alight on salient points. To reiterate: the prime task is to be sufficiently convincing and catalytic: to set Hamlet on a headlong path.

"Now then, note, Watson, that it is Horatio who signals to Hamlet the ghost's entry: 'Look, my lord, it comes.' It is Horatio who interprets the ghost's gestures for the Prince, and when Hamlet asks what should be done, Horatio replies as if speaking on behalf of the apparition: 'It beckons you to go away with it, as if it some impartment did desire to you alone.'

"Horatio is leading the Prince along – he must make sure that Hamlet can be alone with the spectral impersonator. Then after quite skilfully playing the role of caring friend, pretending at first to advise the Prince not to follow or perhaps even half-heartedly holding him back, he detains Marcellus – who is keen to accompany and protect the Prince – long enough for the ghost to deliver its powerful message in peace to Hamlet alone.

"It is critical that Hamlet feel that he, and only he, is privy to his father's secret. And why? First, to enhance the singularity of the event for the Prince, to consecrate the special sense of mission. Secondly, to avoid complications: if word got out, Claudius might be forewarned by rumours and would therefore have had ample time to defend himself and defuse them.

"It was most delicate, I warrant, Watson. One small slip and the game would be given away. But imagine the artistry it took to choreograph the scene. Where would the ghost appear, where would he walk, where could he remain visible yet just out of reach in the dead of night as the crash of the sea sounded. It was beautiful, Watson, beautiful – an incomparable piece of drama.

"It is quite some time before Horatio and Marcellus arrive to find their lord. The ghost has woven his tale, charged Hamlet to avenge him, and already bidden *adieu*. And then the *coup de grace*. Hamlet – and one can only imagine the frantic charged state he was in – orders his companions to swear secrecy. He does not of course divulge the particulars of the ghost's message, but instead warns his companions to 'o'ermaster' their desire to know what has passed privately between himself and the figure. And he adjures them not to reveal what they have seen. Horatio has succeeded completely: Hamlet, deems the ghost 'honest'.

"The now unseen figure – and whether it was the actor's spontaneous improvisation or, as I think more likely, Horatio's perverse brilliance – joins in the command, crying 'Swear!' Thrice, Watson – to seal Hamlet's resolve. It was a masterstroke, a pure masterstroke.

"Horatio's work is essentially complete. He has set the stage – if you will permit me the metaphor – for Hamlet to wreak havoc. It thus becomes merely a waiting game. Horatio has simply to stick to the Prince like a surgeon's plaster in the guise of faithful companionship to make sure Hamlet remains on task.

"Oh, there were a few tense moments to be sure. Claudius proved a formidable foe: had he succeeded in having Hamlet killed in England, Fortinbras' enterprise might have been lost altogether. Fortunately the wily Hamlet outwitted his intended murderers and his unexpected return to Denmark led to the showdown with Claudius, now so desperate as to employ Laertes to do the deed.

"But by this time Claudius has lost. Even if he survived Hamlet, his wife, the Queen, would have been catapulted into inconsolable grief and suspicions would have been raised. Fortinbras would have marched on behalf of the late Prince's factions clamouring for justice – by all accounts Hamlet was beloved of the populace, who would gladly have followed an avenger.

"As it turned out Fortinbras had simply and 'coincidentally' to appear just as the Danish royalty had all expired – Claudius, Gertrude and Hamlet. The treacherous Laertes, of course, also lay dead. Hamlet had earlier dispatched his father Polonius, a member of the Privy Council, who, had he been alive, might perhaps have mustered a defence of the state.

"But Horatio survived – and to the very end he played his duplicitous role: 'Good night, sweet prince, and flights of angels sing thee to thy rest'. The irony, Watson, the incomparable irony.

"Just moments before this sanctimonious ejaculation he pretends to wish to join the Prince by dying with him – by drinking of the poisonous cup, saying 'I am more an antique Roman than a Dane'. Antique Roman indeed. Which one, Watson, which Roman – Brutus, who betrayed Caesar? Cassius, who betrayed Brutus? Caesar, who betrayed all of Rome?

"Horatio recovers rather quickly and would make any of our politicians today blush by his *volte-face*, his seamless assumption of oracular authority: somehow he is perfectly prepared to 'speak to th' yet unknowing world' – quite composed, I should say, for someone who has just witnessed the murder of his dearest friend.

"In the Danish court of Fortinbras would Horatio arrange the King's entertainments – compose the dramas that would grace the court, record and celebrate for posterity the exploits of the new monarch?"

"So is this the motive, Holmes?"

"Perhaps, my friend – men are moved to evil by many things. Several motives typically join together, even if there is one overriding determinant. The tubercle bacillus is the *sine qua non* of tuberculosis, but it requires several ancillary conditions to allow for the disease to effloresce. I am inclined to believe that Horatio loved the fair Ophelia – how carefully he observed and reported on her mental state. She was of his station, Watson, not royalty. It must have been excruciating for him to follow her plight, to see her waste herself on a man who simply for reasons of state could never have cemented a marital alliance – not to mention a man who would murder both her father and brother. I suppose he did not foresee these eventualities – the death of his beloved and her family; but once the cataclysm was let loose it was uncontrollable. Perhaps Horatio suffered – or perhaps not. One cannot know. But these are merely speculations, Watson – though interesting, they are completely irrelevant."

Holmes relaxed at last, puffing quietly on his pipe, the gleam of accomplishment burnishing his brow. I sat in profound appreciative amazement.

"Holmes, you have outdone yourself ... I cannot wait to look over the text."

"Do so, Watson – and then I will rely on your powers for the exposition of this, my crowning achievement, to the world. Any questions, my friend?"

"At the moment, Holmes, just one. Do you have any idea about the significance of the name 'Horatio'? It certainly does not sound Danish."

"An excellent question, Watson, and one, even though the matter is peripheral, I believe I may answer. Edward de Vere

– the true Shakespeare – had a cousin by the same name, and to him was vouchsafed the duty of reporting his cause aright to the unsatisfied – of revealing to the world the actual identity of the magnificent author behind the plays and poems.

"Alas, de Vere must have known that his cousin would betray him – that he would succumb to the pressures of the English court to keep sequestered this most wonderful of secrets. Horatio de Vere, by his cowardly silence, betrayed his relative as basely as Horatio betrayed Hamlet."

Suddenly Holmes sprang up as if stung by an errant bee.

"Watson," he exclaimed, "we must make haste: tonight is the village concert at the vicarage. Come, man, grab a slice of bread and an apple – we will have time later for a true meal."

Holmes snatched his violin and overcoat and I followed his lead without demur, trundling off down the road with him towards the village. He explained that an entertainment had been organised to benefit the parish, and he had agreed to participate.

"Just a few more minutes, Watson, and we will be there," Holmes advised breathlessly.

Indeed, we soon entered the hall and took up positions at the rear. Holmes leaned towards me and whispered, "We have made it in time, thankfully – I am next."

On stage a piece of vaudeville was being enacted – woefully, I must say. Though I myself am as fond as another of a good cross-talk act, the spectacle before me was an absolute shambles. Two listless players, dressed in check suits and green beards, and wielding umbrellas, went through the motions as sullenly as a pair of anaesthetised oxen. It was excruciating to witness.

Sussex was famous for its produce, and apparently the

local youth, crowded with us at the back of the auditorium, had stuffed their pockets with harvest. They stirred restlessly and it took but one tomato to hasten the vaudevillians off stage, mercifully cutting short their tepid exchange.

Now an athletic red-faced clergyman bounded up and putting a best-face forward urged the crowd to calm themselves, for there was 'much more entertainment in store'. He then proceeded to put in a word for restoration of the church organ.

"The Reverend Grant," Holmes murmured. I nodded absently, musing how lucky he was to have captured a wife like Mrs Grant and wondering about his hidden virtues as he droned on.

Before I knew it Holmes had slipped away with his instrument and I was shuddering in horror at the possibilities. Much as I had been moved by the mournful sonata that greeted me on arrival at Holmes cottage, much as I had relished Massenet's *Meditation from Thais*, I could scarcely imagine a rural crowd like this one responding with courtesy.

Yet there on stage was Holmes, joined by the lovely Mrs Grant at the piano. I found myself trembling as the gaunt Holmes took his time tuning the Stradivarius, and hoping against hope that age would command respect. A low murmur of frustration and restlessness began to mount, but with a sudden and simple nod to his bewitching accompanist, Holmes launched ferociously into a lightning-fast rendition of the jazz number *Exactly Like You*.

The audience – and I – were stunned by its speed, zest and unexpected verve. The infectious rhythmic interplay between piano and violin had even the rougher youths tapping their feet uncontrollably. I remember hearing the piece rendered by a gipsy band in Paris years ago, but Holmes and Mrs Grant proved far more captivating. Holmes' bow flashed and an occasional glance at his accompanist, her eyes returning mirthful fire, confirmed the deep musical intimacy they shared. Holmes' *method* was paying off in spades.

The audience erupted in spontaneous acclaim, but before it could swell further Holmes had begun a rendition of *Sonny Boy* that hushed us and when finished left not a dry eye in the house. The silence at the conclusion of the song was palpable, but again Holmes – with the beautifully supportive Mrs Grant – shattered our contemplative repose with a rousing performance of *Rule Britannia* that brought all those sitting to their feet and drew whistles and cheers and stomps from the standees.

Holmes held Mrs Grant's exquisite hand in his own for a single joint bow. While the audience clamoured for encores the Reverend reappeared from the wings to introduce the next performer, inadvertently sending the piano stool crashing into the front row.

By now Holmes had made his way surreptitiously back to me while the crowd was distracted and tugged at my sleeve, counselling silence as he pulled me outside. He mopped his brow and confessed that the performance was one of the most harrowing public challenges he had ever faced. In the foyer he introduced me to a solid-looking man, the very epitome of courteous respectability and gravitas, whom I had spied offering some sort of encouragement to a slim younger gentleman now heading with apparent trepidation towards the very stage on which Holmes has acquitted himself so admirably. I scanned the concert programme and noted that *Sonny Boy* would be repeated a number of times.

"Watson," said Holmes, "please allow me to introduce the gentleman whose trenchant observation in Vienna led to my inquiry into *Hamlet*. I have promised him in advance the very first edition of your account."

"It would be a great honour," the man intoned, "to peruse it. From what Mr Holmes has already told me, it should change forever the way *Hamlet* is played and perceived and bring renewed interest and appreciation. But if you will excuse me, I believe my services are required post-haste."

So saying, the man oozed away imperceptibly as the last notes of a pleasant baritone were greeted by warm applause. I wondered, however, how the gallery would respond to the many subsequent renditions of *Sonny Boy* as the evening wore on. Holmes and I did not linger to find out.

The cool night air on the walk back to the cottage was refreshing. Mrs Grant being otherwise engaged, we rather merrily gathered scraps for a meal. Holmes was understandably spent. His intellectual effort had cost him enormously, and it was a miracle for him to maintain energy for a musical display – and a musical display of such invigorating energy on top of it all.

"I had promised Mrs Grant," confided Holmes, "a special favour from an atheist".

We supped in silence. My mind was galvanised by the most intense curiosity. All of Holmes' startling revelations, observations and opinions clamoured for investigation, and though I needed to return to London first thing in the morning, my presence being required for a ceremony honouring my most recent literary effort, a work of fiction, I yearned to delve into *Hamlet* and to test Holmes' theories.

Holmes furnished me with an unmarked and un-annotated copy of the play before bidding me good night.

"We shall meet for an early breakfast, as I know you must make haste for the city, Watson. I hope though that you will have time tonight to consider my views and render an opinion in the morning."

"With certainty, Holmes – I am accustomed to working late, as you know, and I feel confident I will be able to assess your remarkable interpretation."

"An objective assessment, Watson, is all I ask. Do not let our friendship interfere with your cool judgment. Good night."

My fingers shook as I smoothed the cover of perhaps the greatest artistic work spawned by the mind of a human being. My heart raced and my breaths came in brief gasps as I contemplated my mission. Out of the immediate sphere of Holmes' presence my thinking was already clearer, cooler and lighter. His personality was a difficult one to resist. So used had I been to his correctness that at one time I would have treated any of his assertions, no matter how outlandish, as gospel. Not so now.

Age had brought me a bit of wisdom, and the world had begun to recognise me independently of Holmes. Our talents were different, though complementary, and I do not think I am being immodest to say that in my own sphere mine were the equal of his.

As a physician I was naturally keen to acknowledge the possibility – I do not, in Holmes' case, say *probability* – of a deterioration in mental acuity attendant upon passage into the ninth decade of life. Holmes asked for my sober judgment and I would give him no less. A calm now enveloped me as I sat and prepared to enter the world of Holmes' *Hamlet*.

The night proved unforgettable.

The rich depth of Shakespeare's indelible drama smote me. How many times had I seen it on the stage, yet how different, how much more rich, resonant and powerful it seemed now.

I took nothing for granted. I weighed each word and I allowed myself to be transported by the visceral imagery that only the inimitable language of Shakespeare could convey.

As Holmes said, the play treated of nearly everything. It was indeed a world unto itself – so much so that it dawned upon me that the characters within this world seemed far more real than those of the flesh. I immersed myself in it, and I recognised that the familiar was now cast in a wholly new light. The character I – all of us – had taken for granted all these years – sprang into relief and was impossible to disavow. Far from being the one-dimensional servant, Horatio, in his understated occult malevolence overtook the story. Irony surpassed irony. The *casual* utterances hitherto understood as facilitating dramatic action or merely informing the audience were seen to be pregnant with as yet untold and unappreciated significance.

As Holmes had predicted, once one began simply to entertain the notion that Horatio was more than he seemed, the mystery of the play was unlocked.

The timing of Horatio's arrival at Elsinore, the goading banter with which he greets Hamlet (quite out of place for a poor student addressing his lord), his truly 'truant disposition' to be sure, the way in which Horatio assumes such commanding responsibility in interpreting the ghost's presence to the guards and then to Hamlet himself – the cumulative weight of such things could no longer be ignored or dismissed.

How could Horatio, a poor scholar and by no means a soldier, have been so courageous in the ghost's presence? In fact, in everything involving the ghost, Horatio plays a part: as if to make sure the ghost's message is delivered and properly understood, as he had devised.

The *real* tragedy of Hamlet emerged – the Prince's blindness to betrayal from a completely unseen quarter. Horatio successfully ingratiates himself into the Prince's utter trust. And just as the late King Hamlet could not foresee the betrayal of his brother Claudius, so Prince Hamlet cannot even imagine infidelity from his poor schoolfellow, whom he ironically considered 'as just a man as e'er my conversation cop'd withal'. And when Hamlet, after narrowly escaping murder on the voyage to England, confides by letter to Horatio and signs it 'He that thou knowest thine' – nothing could be truer or more poignant. For indeed Hamlet has been possessed by Horatio, that impoverished commoner who has only his 'good spirits' to recommend himself.

My very soul had been shaken. I saw with utter clarity now that Horatio wore throughout the play merely the trappings and suits of friendship, and I began to imagine, in my mind's eye, how I might create a persuasive narrative for the public. Holmes was quite right to entrust me with this effort. Few would be able to follow his own relatively austere manner of exposition. No, it would take great literary skill and a certain amount of dramatic colour to demonstrate these truths.

I also envisioned, as a result of this evidence, an actor of tremendous restraint, subtlety and commanding presence, to play this incredible villain. I could see such a personage imbuing lines that until now were considered throwaways with profound hidden malevolence. Those simple comments, questions and gestures, assumed for centuries to be straightforward and innocuous, would now begin to tell of greater depths and far more poignant tragedy. The heart of *Hamlet's* mystery had been plucked and I saw nothing less than a revolution at the *Old Vic. Cui bono* indeed!

Only at one point did I begin to waver – when the ghost appears while Hamlet is with his mother the Queen – and then I remembered Holmes' sage remark to the effect that the uncorroborated vision represented a projection of Hamlet's psyche. Yes, when others could see or hear the ghost, it meant that Horatio's prop was in place. Surely the Bard did not intend to make his own wily dramatic stratagems transparent.

The hours of night passed in a flash and I was barely aware of the arrival of dawn. I hadn't slept, but I felt refreshed beyond measure. I surrendered to the joy of speculation. David's famous painting seized me and set my imagination to the inevitable pact between Fortinbras and Horatio – did they meet on some desolate wind-buffeted escarpment in Norway, or in a quiet room at court to seal their agreement, to exchange oaths? Would Fortinbras have Horatio killed after he assumed control of Denmark, or would he have awarded Horatio with a post that suited his devious histrionic talents?

My brain was brimful of ideas and I was eager to return to London, to the comforts of my study where I would do Holmes justice and cause no little upheaval in the literary establishment. Though we were aged, Holmes and I, we yet had vigour within our bosoms!

Monday, 18th July 1938

"**W**ell, Watson," Holmes' suave voice queried as we sat to breakfast, "have you reached a verdict? By the way, I must apologise if the victuals do not equal yesterday's – Mrs Grant is occupied at the moment and I have been left to my own devices."

I smiled and, being so overtaken by emotion, leapt to embrace my age-old companion. Holmes seemed momentarily stunned – his was not an openly affectionate nature – but he recovered sufficiently to relax.

"Guilty as charged!" I exclaimed.

I then proceeded, much to Holmes' obvious delight, to outline my plans to present his case. He grinned appreciatively.

"You see, Watson, how wise I am to entrust this to you. I myself would be of no use – I would bore the reader with detail an lose him in exegesis."

"Well, Holmes, your discovery is enough to bring even greater fame. As before, I am merely the chronicler."

"Fame is not what I seek, Watson. Would I be labouring here in the lap of obscurity if I did? No, it is not fame, my dear friend …"

Holmes gazed dreamily and seemed somewhat melancholy as well, and I was reminded of the sonata he played days before.

"Ah, Watson, what a piece of work is man – if I may borrow a phrase. In even the most loving embrace, the most generous intimacy, there is selfishness and the propensity to betray –the hallmark of *la condition humaine*, I suppose."

He broke out of his strange reverie and gazed at me earnestly, speaking softly.

"I can't thank you enough, my dear fellow. You must know that. Let me keep you no longer from the metropolis – you have a *soirée* to attend, do you not?"

"A small thing, Holmes," I blushed, "after which I will set myself at once to the task of enlightening the world with your wisdom."

We embraced warmly – Holmes had thawed considerably – and I set off down the gravel path leading away from the cottage I knew I might never see again. The scent of the herb garden once again overtook me and flooded me with memories of my military days. The station was minutes away and my train did not leave for half an hour. How it was that I found myself taking a detour towards the greenhouse I cannot rightly explain. Nevertheless I hastened towards it, stealthily.

It was much larger than I had surmised, extending a full thirty yards in length and at least a dozen in width. I pressed my face to the panes along its front and within I could see were nestled row after row of pea plants. I surveyed them quickly but comprehensively, immensely relieved that *Erythroxylum coca* was not among them, for I knew too well of Holmes' troubles in the past. Thankfully all was as it should be, and I upbraided myself for harbouring such doubts about my friend. But as I turned to resume my journey I heard a rustle and I thought I detected motion towards the rear of the edifice.

I immediately crouched and passed noiselessly down the greenhouse's length, taking care barely to breathe. I saw that this smaller rear section was separated in the interior by glass doors from the section housing the pea plants. Its upper half was screened like a porch of sorts. Its entire character was noticeably different – fragrant flowering plants were hung throughout, and candles of various sizes stood along the ledges bordering its inner perimeter. Low to the ground appeared to be a large bed strewn with heaps of coloured pillows. It resembled nothing so much as a kind of boudoir.

Then she stirred and my feet turned to stone.

Mrs Grant rose languidly, so beautiful and radiant with youthful morning joy, and stretched her unclothed body with consummate unconscious grace. I tried to flee but remained rooted, transfixed, confused, embarrassed, and unable to pull myself away from such captivating and inimitable splendour. Her slender arms reached upwards and back to smooth her long soft hair. She stepped quietly towards a yellow rose in the gentle early light of day and plucked a petal with her lips.

Then to my indescribable horror I spied, on a small oak table adjacent to the bed, a familiar pipe.

Sherlock Holmes
and the
Belgravian Letter

Roger Jaynes

About the Author

Roger Jaynes has spent his entire life writing about a multitude of subjects in a variety of ways. As an award-winning sportswriter for the *Miami Herald, Gannett News Service* and *The Milwaukee Journal*, he was the recipient of over forty-five national writing awards including his being chosen as the top 'Sports News Writer of The Year' in the United States by the Associated Press Sports Editors Association in 1977.

After leaving journalism in 1988, Roger served as the Director of Public Relations at Road America, the largest motor sports road course in North America, and at the same time continued to be a contributor to numerous magazines, including *Inside Sports, Indy Car Magazine* and *Auto Racing Digest*. From 1999 to 2003 he served as Vice President, Corporate Communications, at the Experimental Aircraft Association, which annually hosts the largest recreational aviation event in the world.

Roger has also written an Indy car novel, *Speedway*, and currently lives in Oshkosh, WI, with his wife Mary.

By the same author

Sherlock Holmes: A Duel with the Devil

Sherlock Holmes and the Chilford Ripper

ONE

August of 1895, as I recall, was unusually warm for the time of year, a wearying succession of simmering, sunlit afternoons that caused the air to hang heavily and close about our Baker Street lodgings. Although the tepid evenings brought some relief, the unseasonable heat still at times made the smallest task seem a mighty chore, and the slightest movement an inconvenience. Sleep on those sullen nights was fitful at best.

The dry summer had also been, for my good friend and associate Mr Sherlock Holmes, an unusually active period of time – during which he was presented with a long series of cases. While some were of greater interest than others, the list included many which were both intriguing and bizarre, including the investigation of the death of Captain Peter Carey[1] in July, and the sinister schemes of Mr Jonas Oldacre of Norwood[2], which Holmes had uncovered and put right only the week before.

To seek relief from our stuffy confines, Holmes and I often

---

[1] The Adventure of Black Peter
[2] The Adventure of the Norwood Builder

undertook a leisurely walk after dining, alternately strolling in the direction of Hyde Park, or toward Regent's Park, and then back again. On this particular night, however, our spirits were too wilted to attempt even that. The intense heat of the afternoon had also dulled our appetites. The excellent dinner provided by Mrs Hudson sat scarcely touched upon our table, and our wine glasses remained half full.

Holmes, after a few bites, had retired listlessly to his velvet armchair, where he now lay motionless, his eyes closed as if in sleep. Taking to my chair, I began making my way through *The Evening Standard,* pausing occasionally to glance towards the open window, through which I could hear the resonant clip-clop of passing cabs below and occasional voices in the street. Each time, I also hoped to catch some slight movement of breeze upon the curtain that might herald relief. Alas, in vain. So great was my discomfort that, after a moment or two, I allowed myself the informality of unfastening my collar and loosening my tie.

"Have you found anything of interest, Watson?" Holmes asked at length, opening his eyes slowly.

I knew, as always, that his inquiry referred purely to matters of a criminal nature, rather than any other major events that had taken place.

"It does seem to have been a busy day," I replied, as I scanned the page before me. "Three stabbings have been reported. Two, it says here, occurred as a result of altercations in public houses in the East End, and the third in a house of ill repute on Bolton Row."

Holmes cast a knowing glance in my direction.

"The world's oldest profession has never been without its element of danger," he declared with a sigh. "Who did the stabbing then? The woman or her client?"

"It was the client. The victim claims that he was attacked for no apparent reason."

A faint smile crossed my companion's lips.

"Reason enough, I'll wager, since he surely paid in advance. Go on."

"Yes, here we are. A china shop on Bond Street was broken into late this morning, but according to this report, the police quickly apprehended the fellow, with the stolen goods in hand. There also have been numerous residential thefts reported, and no less than half a dozen muggings in the street."

I continued to hurriedly scan the rows of type before me, hoping to find some report that might spark my good friend's interest.

"Hello! Here are two intriguing items. Someone impersonating a groom has stolen a horse in the Old Kent Road. And a man named Henry Gilham has jumped into the Thames from Waterloo Bridge."

Holmes guffawed.

"Seeking relief from the heat, no doubt," he remarked dryly.

"No, no. It was, the police say, an attempted suicide. Gilham, after being pulled from the water, claimed his wife had ceased to love him, taken up with an insurance salesman from Brixton and moved to parts unknown."

Holmes rolled his eyes with disinterest.

"Ah, well then," he commented, "I guess that does explain it." With great effort, my friend roused himself to a sitting position, and then reached down for his favourite black clay and the Persian slipper, which he had left lying amidst the scattered remnants of the morning papers beside his chair.

"I cannot say, however, that this continued flurry of

criminal activity is at all surprising."

"And why is that?" I asked.

A look of incredulity crossed Holmes' long, gaunt face.

"My dear Watson," he insisted, as he filled his pipe, "surely you must be aware that the rate of crime always rises in direct proportion to the clime of the season? It is, after all, a proven fact." Holmes struck a match, and inhaled deeply, sending thick blue clouds of smoke spiralling towards the ceiling. "I have, I'm certain, completed a short monograph on the subject. Would you care to read it? It documents my position thoroughly."

Accustomed as I was to my friend's unorthodox ways, I could not help but be amused by his remarks.

"My dear fellow," I scoffed, "I cannot believe for a moment that you are serious. Why, a check of every police blotter in London would show that crimes of every conceivable nature occur all year round in this great city."

"Quite so," Holmes concurred evenly, "and it would also show, as my research so clearly proves, that the frequency of said crimes rises steadily to a peak and then trails off again, in the months between the vernal and autumnal equinoxes."

In spite of Holmes' stern rejoinder, I remained sceptical of it all.

"And why, pray tell, is that?" I asked.

Holmes looked at me impatiently, as if I was a schoolchild who somehow could not understand why two plus two made four.

"There are two reasons, Watson," he explained, with a sigh. "As a medical man, I assumed you would easily deduce the first."

"And that is?"

"The first is physiological. As temperature and humidity

rise, they have the worst possible effects upon the human condition. The blood becomes warm. Hubris and passion run high. Patience and forbearance, on the other hand, weaken markedly. So it is only natural then, in situations of stress, that the baser of man's instincts more often come to the fore. Hence, the incidences of violent crimes – assault, stabbings, murder and so forth increase."

"And the other reason?" I pressed, determined to carry this through.

Holmes smiled, and contentedly sent another spiral of pipe smoke rising.

"A much simpler one, to be sure. It is called accessibility. When the heat of summer becomes oppressive, the citizenry of this great metropolis quite naturally avail themselves more to the out-of-doors to seek relief."

I frowned.

"I am sorry, Holmes," I declared, "but I do not see the connection."

"You see, but you do not observe, Watson. In a balmy clime, windows are constantly left open. Doors, which see more frequent use, are more likely to remain unlocked. Far more people take to the streets and parks for increased periods of time, especially in the evenings. All of which puts both people and their possessions within easier reach of the criminal element. The result is an accompanying increase in the lesser crimes, such as mugging, theft, or the mere picking of a pocket. Harsh weather, on the other hand, demands by necessity that Londoners remain more often within the safety of their dwellings. Doors and windows are routinely locked and tightly shut. Likewise, criminals themselves are not as apt to be about in the cold and wet – unless the reward is unusually great."

Holmes shrugged and gave me an amused look.

"The facts, you must admit, Watson," he concluded, "speak for themselves." He threw up his hands. "It is all quite absurdly simple."

He was right, of course, I knew. Given that, I resigned myself to do what I had oft-times done before in similar situations – beat a hasty, yet graceful, retreat from the subject at hand.

"Well, there is most certainly something to what you say," I admitted, returning my attention to the paper before me. "I shall be interested in asking Lestrade his opinion the next time he calls ... "

At that instant, our conversation was interrupted by the jangle of our front doorbell below, followed by Mrs Hudson's shrill protestations and a decidedly heavy tread upon our stair. To my surprise Holmes rose up quickly from his chair straightening his shirt and tails. A faint smile was upon his lips.

"You mentioned our friend, Lestrade," he commented. "By the footstep, I do believe it is he."

Instinctively, I glanced at the rounded clock upon our mantel.

"In that case, he has certainly chosen an inopportune time to call," I replied, wearily pulling myself to my feet as well. "It is, after all, nearly half past ten."

"Then certainly, it must be a matter of some importance," Holmes surmised as we heard a harsh knock upon the door.

"Lestrade is not a man in the habit of making social calls. Show him in, will you? Ah, good evening, my dear Lestrade. And what, pray tell, brings you to our lodgings at this late hour?"

At first, the lean policeman did not answer, as he stood

before us, his familiar hat clutched tightly in his hands. His darting eyes, I observed, presaged trouble, and his ferret-like features, which seemed to lurk behind his thick black moustache, were unusually grim. It was clear that he was in some distress.

"A very sticky affair, Mr Holmes," he finally answered gravely, as he stepped inside. From his pocket he drew a handkerchief and mopped beads of moisture from his brow. "And that's no pun intended."

Holmes waved him to have a seat, but Lestrade refused.

"How so?" my friend inquired.

"Sir Arthur Wilcox has been found shot dead in his home at Cadogan Place," the policeman declared. "Murdered and, worse yet, robbery as well."

"Wilcox, the Principal Private Secretary to the Prime Minister!" I exclaimed. "But this is a tragedy for the new Government, surely. He was Lord Salisbury's confidential assistant, as I understand, and a personal friend of both Balfour and Lansdowne[3]."

"You are correct," Lestrade stated, as he dabbed his forehead once again. "He was to have departed London for Greece on Tuesday next to represent Her Majesty's Government at the Athens conference, which begins upon the fifth."

Holmes strode to the fireplace and put out his pipe.

"I am somewhat familiar with the particulars," he remarked. "According to my brother Mycroft, if matters are

---

[3] Lord Salisbury had formed his third Government in the June of 1895 naming Lord Lansdowne as Secretary of State for War, and Sir Arthur James Balfour as First Lord of the Treasury and Leader of the House of Commons.

not put right, our relationships with no less than three Mediterranean countries may suffer. Such was the import of the matter, that Salisbury insisted that Sir Arthur represent us."

"Sad to say," Lestrade continued, "it is a commission he will never undertake. He was found at his desk not one hour ago, a bullet in his brain."

"And you believe robbery is the motive?"

The policeman hesitated.

"It would seem so," he stated. "A wall safe in Sir Arthur's study was found open, and the terrace doors as well." Lestrade shifted his hat uneasily from one hand to the other. "I am on my way to the scene of the crime at this very moment. I had hoped, given the nature of the case, that you might care to accompany me and lend an unofficial hand, so to speak."

An amused look crossed my companion's lean face. He had, over the years, become accustomed to such entreaties of assistance from Lestrade – with the proviso that Scotland Yard received the credit for any success. Given that, I was not at all displeased when Holmes turned on his heel and strode silently to the fireplace, allowing the dour Inspector another moment's consternation before replying.

"In a case of this import," he replied finally, with just the right touch of solicitude, "how could you imagine I might refuse? As in the past, you may rely completely upon our discretion. What say you, Doctor? Are you game for such a nocturnal adventure?"

"I can think of nothing better," I answered, quickly reaching for a notebook and pen. "Shall I bring my revolver?"

Holmes knocked the ashes of his pipe into the grate, and grabbed up his magnifying glass from the drawer.

"In this case, I doubt we shall need it," he determined. As we made for the door he glanced at me. "However, I do suggest you do something about your tie."

Minutes later we were clattering south through the gas-lit streets in a Scotland Yard four-wheeler, at which time Lestrade gave us his account of the few facts he possessed.

"I was contacted by the Foreign Office not half an hour ago," he explained tersely. "I have been personally instructed, as you might expect, to handle this matter as discreetly as possible. Given the delicate nature of Sir Arthur's mission, Fleet Street must not have a field day with this news."

"Has the Prime Minister has been informed?" Holmes asked pointedly.

"Straight away. Whitehall is concerned that certain documents – compromising documents, I might add – may well have been stolen. An inquiry is already under way to determine what papers Sir Arthur might have had in his possession."

Holmes raised a thoughtful finger to his lips. In the glow of the passing street lamps, I could see his dark eyes gleaming with anticipation; his earlier lethargy had vanished. The sudden change, I knew, was because he had once again been thrust into his proper element, confronted by a crime so horrible that it challenged his remarkable powers of intellect and deduction.

"On the eve of so important a conference, diplomatic theft must certainly be considered," he declared. "It is, at least, a logical starting point for our investigation, until we acquire more data."

"Perhaps," Lestrade remarked ruefully," but you must admit, it would be better all round should our thief turn out to be a common Johnny. Some chap who has made off with jewellery or the family silver. As I see it, that's the real rub here. What is our motive, Mr Holmes? Are we dealing with ordinary theft, or espionage?" The lean policeman squirmed. "Tell me the former, and I shall certainly breathe much easier."

"Your point is well taken, Lestrade," Holmes replied, "but it is too early to form an opinion. Common theft, certainly, cannot be discounted. Sir Arthur, I have no doubt, was a man of considerable means. It is not hard to imagine that valuables of some sort were kept inside his safe, or that his death occurred when he came upon the robbery in progress."

"That is a line of reasoning I pray proves correct," the policeman agreed. "A common crime, you must agree, would be the best the Government could hope for in this matter."

Holmes' face was grim.

"It would be nothing short of a miracle," he concluded. "For if this is a theft of a political nature, we will indeed be hard pressed to put things right."

At Oxford Street, we turned past Marble Arch and swung south along the eastern edge of Hyde Park, where crowds had gathered upon the lawns and public benches, taking in the pleasant night air. Throngs of people were in the streets as well, and traffic at the crossings was unusually heavy. In the area beneath Wellington's memorial the scene was festive, with vendors hawking ginger beer and ices, and children dancing to an old man's hurdy-gurdy. One industrious fellow had even erected a telescope atop a small wooden platform, offering views of the stars for only a penny.

Normally, such gaiety would have lightened my mood, but I felt myself too overwhelmed by the sombreness and import of our present journey to respond. Instead, as the orange lights of Saint George's Hospital came into view, I found myself hoping, like Lestrade, that matters of the Crown had not been compromised by this current tragedy.

"You would think that it was Guy Fawkes night," I observed lamely, "with all these people roaming about ..."

"Criminals, too, quite likely," Lestrade interjected. "I'll wager the district stations will be especially busy tonight, Doctor. Why, there is not a mugger or pickpocket worth his salt who would pass up working such crowds as these."

There was no need to look; I could almost feel Holmes' heavy gaze upon me.

"The good Inspector has made a valid point," he declared with satisfaction, as he stared off into the starry night. "It is, indeed, on nights such as this that street crime flourishes. What a pity that such misguided souls choose to live off the hardship of others." He shrugged his shoulders in resignation. "*C'est la vie.*"

Traffic lightened as we continued west on Knightsbridge, a street of tall houses, ornate hotels, and singularly fashionable shops which marked the northern boundary of Belgravia, a district whose aristocratic stucco mansions were occupied by some of the wealthiest and most influential members of both Houses of Parliament. A sudden sense of historical presence surged through me. Many embassies, I knew, were located in this area. Albert Gate is adjacent to the French Embassy while Belgrave Square is home to the Austrian Embassy, with the American and Spanish legations being located nearby. Might the results of our efforts this night, I wondered, have some effect on what transpired within those very walls on the morrow?

"You know, Holmes," I remarked, "I have a decided intuition that this matter may, in fact, be of great importance.

Not unlike the problem we handled for my old friend Phelps[4], you may recall?"

"The overtones of this case are already much more sinister, Watson," my friend replied. "A great man's blood has been shed."

Lestrade stroked his dark moustache nervously.

"If important documents are missing, gentlemen," he intoned, "then I feel Mr Holmes' assessment may prove correct. We shall certainly be up against it. We must only hope that is not the case."

---

[4] The Naval Treaty

TWO

The wheels of our carriage rounded the curb into the secluded, tree-lined avenue that was Cadogan Place. The Wilcox residence was an imposing two-story structure looming behind large iron gates at the end of the street, with tall chimneys that poked above the trees into the moonlit sky. As we approached, I observed lights showing from the ground floor windows, while the second story appeared dark. Two of Scotland Yard's four-wheelers stood unattended in the drive. Otherwise, nothing appeared amiss.

As we stepped down, a uniformed constable suddenly appeared out of the shadows, rapidly advancing in our direction.

"Can I be of help to you gentlemen?" he asked firmly. Then noticing the police markings on our cab, he snapped to attention.

"Sorry, Inspector," he said to Lestrade. "I didn't realise it was you."

"Right you are, Bennett," Lestrade affirmed smartly. "This is Sherlock Holmes and Doctor Watson. They are assisting me in this affair."

"Very good, Inspector." A flicker of a smile crossed the stocky constable's face. "And I am glad to see you as well," he said to Holmes. "No disrespect, but we all thought the Professor had done you in for quite some time."

"So, quite thankfully, did Colonel Moran[5]," my colleague remarked. "But tell me, what have we here?"

"A tragic business, I'm afraid," the officer replied. "Come this way. Sergeant Potter is inside."

We followed Constable Bennett through the front door and an impressive chandeliered vestibule, which opened into the mansion's spacious main hall. Tall doors of traditional English oak lined both sides of the hall, and at the far end, a wide staircase rose to the upper rooms beyond. The walls, I noticed immediately, were graced with paintings depicting the excitement of the hunt – huge vibrant scenes in which excited groups of red-coated hunters spurred their mounts on through field and forest, following the hounds in pursuit of the elusive fox. Oil lamps flickered brightly from ornate wall mounts, and potted plants, elegant chairs and thick carpets had been strategically placed as in the lobby of a large hotel, obviously to accommodate large numbers of guests at official functions.

Our footsteps echoed as we crossed the immense hall and approached the door of the slain civil servant's study, which was located at the foot of the stairs. Before it, a uniformed constable stood guard, and a second officer, who I took to be Sergeant Potter, was conferring with a large man dressed in a servant's attire. Upon seeing us he said something to the fellow before turning to greet us.

"Good evening, Inspector," Potter said, with a policeman's

---

[5] The Empty House

frown. He nodded towards the study door. "The body is still where it was found. The coroner has been summoned, and I have posted men at the terrace doors – and about the grounds, just in case."

Lestrade gave the sergeant a satisfied nod.

"It does seem you have handled things well," he said officiously. "Although our bird has, quite likely, long since flown. What of Lady Wilcox?"

"She had retired, but apparently was wakened by the shot," Potter said. "She rushed down, I'm told, in a hysterical state." He turned to the big fellow beside him. "Mr Davis here, who discovered the body, was able to restrain her before she entered the study. His wife and the maids then returned her to her bed. Her physician, Doctor Morrison, has only just arrived and is with her now."

Lestrade stiffened, and turned towards the big man.

"And who are you?" he asked, eyeing him pointedly.

"I am the butler, sir. My wife is the cook, and I have served, on occasion, as Sir Arthur's bodyguard as well."

Holmes gestured towards the study door.

"I take it then that nothing has been disturbed?" he asked.

"No, sir," Potter insisted. "I posted my men and locked things tight. I felt it best to wait for the Inspector."

Holmes' countenance brightened.

"Congratulations, Sergeant, you have done well," he assured the officer. "Remarkably so, in fact. I suggest then, Lestrade, that we conduct our investigation immediately, before the coroner and his minions arrive upon the scene."

"Very well," Lestrade replied. He gave the large man another penetrating look. "You will accompany us, Mr Davis. I shall, I am certain, have more questions to ask of you."

Sir Arthur Wilcox's personal study was much less

oppressive than the closeness of the main hall we had just transgressed, thanks to the ventilation of the open doors leading to the terrace that were now guarded by one of London's finest. The huge room was a reflection of both the strength and purpose of the British Empire. Sturdy beams braced its high ceiling, and the paintings upon the walls were of a military motif and included scenes from famous campaigns of the past. Regimental banners stood about the room, cavalry swords hung above the fireplace, and hundreds of volumes filled the tall pedimented bookshelves that dominated the entire chamber. Atop a grand piano, rows of photographs had been displayed – including, I noticed sadly, a signed likeness of the Prime Minister himself – a memento, no doubt, of some happier occasion.

All this, of course, vanished from my consciousness in a heartbeat when I turned to view the ghastly scene of death that lay before us.

In the soft glow of the reading lamps, the renowned civil servant lay slumped across his desk, his right arm hanging limply at his side. He had been shot once, slightly above the right temple, and a rear portion of his skull had been blown away. His eyes were half-open and glazed; his mouth hung slack. Blood-soaked sheets of stationary could be seen beneath him, a large quill pen lay close by, and his inkstand had been knocked aside as well, causing its dark contents to splatter out across the blotter.

It was, by any measure, a horrible sight. I found myself affected quite deeply, for patriotic as well as personal reasons. Sir Arthur had, after all, served his country in various capacities under three Prime Ministers; his loyalty to the Crown was beyond question. Turning away, I shuddered, as I caught sight of a large revolver, lying among dark patches of blood upon the carpeting nearby.

"How awful," I despaired. "This is an unjust fate, you must admit, for such a righteous man."

Lestrade put his hand upon my shoulder in an unusual display of emotion.

"You are right, Doctor," he consoled. "Solving this case cannot undo the injustice of it all."

Holmes said not a word during our exchange. Instead, he frowned and took out his glass, and began to examine the body and the top of the civil servant's desk, while Lestrade and I looked on silently. His cold reaction to it all did not surprise me. Emotion, I had learned over our many years together, played little part in his scheme of things, save when it became a motive for some crime. He felt, in fact, that emotion was in most cases a deterrent to the workings of his highly disciplined mind. 'Logic, Watson,' I often heard him say, 'is an infallible machine that drives the mental processes. If used correctly, it will always produce a correct conclusion'. Would it now, I wondered, or were we too late?

"The cause of death does interest me," my friend finally remarked at length. "What say you then, Watson?"

"My views, of course, would be unofficial," I replied, with some hesitation. "Should we not wait for the coroner?"

"Nonsense," Holmes insisted. "I would value your opinion."

"Very well – with your permission, Lestrade."

Given the Inspector's silent nod I bent down and carefully examined the body.

"It is my opinion that Sir Arthur died of a single gunshot wound to the brain," I stated. "Given the powder marks on his skin, I conclude the shot was administered at close range. By the angle of the trajectory, I doubt the fatal shot was fired from the centre of the room, where the gun in question now lies."

Holmes smiled.

"Ah, yes," he said. "The location of the gun. That is an interesting point."

"Why, there is no mystery to that," Lestrade declared. "The gun was obviously placed there after the fact. Dropped, most likely, as the killer made his escape. Why would he want it, after all? If found on his person, it would only serve to connect him to the act."

"Ah, I see. Your theory then?"

Lestrade puffed out his chest a little before he began.

"It is as clear as crystal," he observed. "No doubt, the thief climbed the trellis and entered through the terrace doors – which were open due to the closeness of the evening. Most likely, he surprised Sir Arthur, who was either engrossed in Government business, or reading at the time ..."

"Reading?" I inquired. "However do you deduce that?"

Lestrade smiled smugly.

"You will note the open book and spectacles on top of the desk," the policeman indicated. He paused a moment before continuing. "The facts speak for themselves, Doctor," he said, with authority. "The thief forced Sir Arthur, at gunpoint, to remove certain documents from the safe, after which he shot him and made good his escape. It is a particularly cold-blooded crime, I do admit. But he could hardly afford to leave a witness."

Again I shuddered as my mind contemplated the scene Lestrade had just described – the famed civil servant sitting helpless at his desk, as the killer ruthlessly raised his gun and fired the fatal shot.

"If what you say is true," I ventured," it indicates

diplomatic thievery, surely. Beyond that the killer was, most likely, a professional assassin."

Lestrade strode across the room to the open wall safe and peered inside.

"Look here!" he cried. "There is no doubt these papers have been disturbed. More documents lie here upon the floor." The policeman's face was grim. "This seems to confirm our worst fears, gentlemen," he said at length. "My guess is that the thief had been observing the house for quite some time – to determine when best to strike, I should imagine."

Holmes gave the interior of the safe a cursory look.

"Mr Davis," he inquired, "was Sir Arthur in the habit of keeping Government documents in this safe?"

"At times, sir," the servant replied. "However, I could not tell you what was there – or what might be missing."

Holmes smiled thinly.

"Yes, that is the vexing point, is it not?" he suggested. "If we knew that, we would not be on such shifting sands."

My friend knelt down and carefully lifted up the weapon.

"An Enfield, large calibre," he observed. "Just the type, I'd say, for a former military man."

Lestrade was quick to pounce upon my friend's remark.

"What of it, Davis?" he inquired fiercely. "Did Sir Arthur possess a revolver of this type?"

For an instant the large man appeared flustered.

"Well, yes, sir, that is I think he did," he admitted. "I do know he kept an Enfield, but of its calibre I cannot be certain. He seldom carried it when I accompanied him, and I have not seen it in some time."

Lestrade eyed the man.

"And where might he have kept it?" he inquired pointedly.

"Again, sir, I cannot say. His bedroom, perhaps."

91

"Or in his desk?" Holmes suggested.

In a flash my friend was at the civil servant's side, quickly opening and closing drawers, one by one. It was, upon his third try, that he uttered a short cry of satisfaction, producing from the drawer a box of cartridges.

"Enfield, thirty-six calibre," he declared. "I think, upon examination, that these will match the weapon in hand." He motioned the Inspector to his side. "You will note, Lestrade, there are six bullets missing from the box."

Lestrade gave him a wary look.

"Are you suggesting," he inquired, "that Wilcox was murdered with his own gun?"

"Given what we see before us, I think it is quite likely," Holmes said dryly. He paused, and thoughtfully put a finger to his lips. "Clearly, this case is more complex than I had imagined."

"Well, it is all quite simple to me," Lestrade insisted. "If that is Sir Arthur's revolver, it only supports my theory."

Holmes arched his eyebrows inquisitively as he replaced the box of cartridges in the drawer.

"And how is that?" he asked.

A smug look crossed Lestrade's face again.

"I am amazed you had to ask," he retorted, "for there is only one possible explanation. Wilcox, obviously, made an attempt for his weapon, but the thief was too quick and disarmed him." Lestrade swung round as if imagining the scene before him.

"Yes," he concluded, clearly pleased with his deductions, "that is exactly how it must have happened. It was a bonus for our intruder, you must admit, to be able to commit the crime with a weapon that could not be traced."

Holmes frowned.

"I suppose that is a possibility," he admitted, "I am not, however, prepared to accept it until I know more of the facts."

Holmes crossed the room, took out his magnifying glass, and closely examined the latches of the terrace doors. Then, while Lestrade and I watched in silence, he strode out onto the terrace, looked over the balustrade for a while, and then returned inside exhibiting a puzzled look upon his face.

"You are correct about the doors," he told Lestrade. "There are no scratches anywhere, nothing to indicate a forced entry. However, if you would indulge me, there is another inspection I desire to make. It will only take a few moments, I assure you – and the loan of Sergeant Potter's bullseye."

Taking the lantern, Holmes darted out into the hall, much to our amazement. It was obvious that he had noticed something we had not.

Lestrade gave me an exasperated look.

"There are times I think your friend is too Machiavellian," he declared. "This is clearly a case of diplomatic theft and murder, just as I described it. The real problem, as I see it, is the recovery of those documents, before they fall into evil hands – if they haven't already. You mark my word, Doctor – it will not be easy keeping a lid on this one. Oh, we can watch the ports and stations, and we can search every passenger, if need be. At this end I'll have extra patrols out within hours. Every stranger will be stopped and searched, but what if the papers have already been passed?" The Inspector gave me a knowing look. "Perhaps to waiting hands, shall we say, in a certain embassy, nearby? If that has happened our hands are tied. Diplomatic pouches, after all, are as sacrosanct as the church ..."

Lestrade's remarks were suddenly interrupted by the shout of voices from the garden; the constable stationed at the terrace doors ran to the balustrade.

"Oy!" he cried, looking down. "What's going on here? Stop, you!"

In an instant we were at his side, peering down on the moonlit garden. What we observed, to our astonishment, was Holmes scaling the vine-covered trellis, swinging the beam from his lantern back and forth before him as he made his way.

Lestrade shook his head in disbelief.

"It is all right!" he called down to the constables below. "It is Mr Holmes. He is here on my behalf."

It took Holmes but another few moments to reach us, at which time he swung himself up and over the balustrade, then returned Sergeant Potter his lantern.

"And what was that all about?" Lestrade demanded, with some exasperation. "You knew I had men in the garden. Did you not expect your theatrics would send up a cry? I take it you are now satisfied – for whatever reason – that a man could climb that trellis."

"On the contrary," Holmes replied. "I am now satisfied that no man ever did."

The policeman appeared perplexed.

"Whatever do you mean?" he asked.

"The trellis is covered with heavy vines," Holmes explained. "Someone as heavy as our assassin could not traverse such shrubbery without breaking a bough or two along the way. And yet, from ground to the terrace wall, all was pristine. Likewise the garden soil, I might add. There was not a footprint to be found."

"That is all very well and good," Lestrade retorted, "but it still doesn't change the basic facts ..."

Holmes silenced him with a steady look and a wave of his

hand. He led us back into the study, where he stood silently for a moment, contemplating I knew not what. But it was clear to me that a theory of some sort was formulating in his mind.

Holmes produced a cigarette and lit it.

"Mr Davis," he inquired, "might you tell us what you know of this unfortunate mishap?"

The large man sighed.

"I know very little," he replied. "Save that it was I who found my master's body. It was about half past eight."

"Continue."

"Sir Arthur had, in recent months, taken to the habit of retiring to his study after dinner – and remaining there unusually late. Only on certain evenings, mind you, but never with regularity. I put it down to his increasing duties, once Lord Salisbury had taken office, since he relied heavily on Sir Arthur's counsel. That, and his reading, of course. He was a vociferous reader, sir."

Holmes picked up the volume that lay beside Sir Arthur's body.

"Aristotle," he commented, as he opened it to a page that had been marked. "Ah, *Nicomachean Ethics* I see. Tell me, Mr Davis, was your master a student of this philosopher?"

"Yes, sir," Davis replied. "Sir Arthur quoted him to others often. Chapter and verse, as you would say."

Holmes smiled.

"For that, I cannot fault him," he told the servant. "Aristotle is the father of deductive reasoning. Be it world politics, or crime in the streets, his lectures do explain everything."

Holmes closed the book and returned it to its place. I could tell, by his expression, that he had come to some sort of important decision in the inner recesses of his inquiring mind.

"And what exactly happened tonight, Davis?" he questioned. "After Sir Arthur had retired to this room?"

"I cannot say," the man replied. He glanced down at Sir Arthur's body, and a steely look came in his eyes. "But I wish that I had been here. God knows, I guarantee you, it would have turned out differently."

Holmes took a puff on his cigarette.

"And you were where?"

"My wife and I were in the kitchen, at the other side of the house, finishing off the dishes and the cleaning, you understand? It was near nine o'clock, as I recall. I decided, that before we retired, to inquire if Sir Arthur desired a final brandy, or perhaps a pot of tea. But when I knocked upon the study door, there was no answer. Naturally, I tried the handle, but it would not move." Davis' eyes widened a little. "The door was clearly locked."

"This was at nine o'clock, you say?" Holmes asked.

"Yes, sir," the butler replied. "Only a minute or two before."

"And what did you do then?"

"I returned to the kitchen, and told Mrs Davis what had happened. 'He's probably fallen asleep,' she told me. 'Go back, and try again'. So back I went. I knocked repeatedly and called my master's name – this time a little louder than before. But still there was no answer ..."

Holmes looked at the man expectantly.

"Except ..."

"Except that this time," Davis said with agitation, "when I tried the door again it swung open wide!"

I thought Lestrade would drop his hat.

"What!" he exclaimed. "Come, come, my man. The door

was unlocked this time, you say?"

"Yes, sir," Davis answered firmly.

"You are certain," Holmes insisted, "that you tried the door firmly the first time you inquired? You are not mistaken upon that point?"

The butler shook his head.

"Absolutely not, sir. I tried it repeatedly, but the handle would not budge. You understand, that was what alarmed me most. Sir Arthur has never been a man to lock his doors, not in all our years together."

Holmes glanced at me alarmingly.

"Then we have indeed stumbled onto a most interesting clue," he concluded. "Now tell me, Davis, how long were you gone?"

Davis pursed his lips while he thought.

"Not more than ten minutes, sir," he said finally. "Not even that much, most likely. As I told you, I returned immediately."

Sherlock Holmes paused a moment before pressing his point.

"Was it long enough," he asked, "for someone to have unlocked the study doors, espied the hall, and then made good his escape? Out of the front door, perhaps, while you and your wife were conferring?"

"That does explain it," Lestrade interrupted, before the butler could answer. "Ten minutes. Why, that is more than enough time for the killer to cross the hall and be gone – just as I suspected."

Holmes demurred as he stared at the open terrace doors.

"And yet, one nagging question does remain," he informed us. "How did the killer enter? Certainly, it was not via the terrace."

Lestrade stroked his dark moustache as he thought.

"Then there is only one possibility," he stated flatly. "He must have entered the same way he left – through the hall." Lestrade's countenance brightened. "Why, of course, don't you see? It all fits together perfectly. The murderer gained entrance through the front hall, then slipped into the study – the doors were unlocked, remember – and he surprised Wilcox from behind."

Holmes made no reply, but by the expression on his face I could see that he was not convinced. He turned again to the butler.

"Pray continue, Mr Davis," he enjoined. "Tell us, if you would, exactly what you saw when you entered this room."

"Just what you see now," the big fellow said sombrely. "The reading lamps were lit, and Sir Arthur was slumped across his desk. I assumed my wife had been correct, and so I tried to rouse him." The butler shuddered. "You can imagine my horror, sir, as I stepped closer and saw the blood, and his eyes staring up at me. It was a sight I shall never forget. I knew immediately that he was dead. Then I saw the wall safe hanging open, and the terrace doors ajar. Next I observed the gun, lying right there where you see it now, stained with blood."

Davis paused before continuing.

"I am not a squeamish man, gentlemen," he said. "As a soldier, I saw death frequently in the Crimea. But to see such a fine man as this brought down ... " He shook his head sadly. "Well, it sickened me to the quick. For a moment, I could not move – I was stunned. Then I composed myself, and left the room. My only thought was to summon the police ..."

"But you were interrupted," Holmes suggested, "by Lady

Wilcox, I believe?"

"You are correct," the butler replied. "Unfortunately, my ordeal was just beginning."

"Continue."

"As I rushed into the hall I heard a low cry, and there was Her Ladyship at the bottom of the stairs. She was in her nightdress, with a stricken look upon her face.

" 'Whatever is the matter, Davis?' she cried. 'I heard you calling my husband's name.'

" 'A terrible thing,' I replied. 'Sir Arthur has been shot. I am about to go for the police'.

" 'Shot!' she shrieked. 'Why, send for a doctor then!'

" 'It is too late for that,' I told her. 'He's in God's hands now'.

"Hearing my words, she rushed towards me. 'Take me to him at once,' she ordered. 'I want to see my husband, do you hear? Take me to him, Davis. Then go, and summon help immediately'.

" 'I cannot do that, My Lady,' I insisted. 'It is not a sight I can allow you to see'.

"It was clear to me, gentlemen, that she was in a panic. Her eyes were wild, like those of a frightened animal. Twice, she tried to force her way past, screaming at me, but I held her firmly by the shoulders and was able to block her way. Fortunately, at that moment, my wife appeared upon the scene and we were able to return Her Ladyship to her room. Once there, she seemed to calm considerably, but I stayed beside her just in case, while my wife aroused the maids. I then sent for the police, and Doctor Morrison as well."

The large man's face wore a look of dismay.

"I have no doubt that my disobedience shall cost me my position – and probably my wife's as well," he concluded sadly, "but I had to do what I thought was best."

My heart went out to the beleaguered man.

"As a physician, I should say you acted wisely," I consoled him. "Given what you have told us, I feel quite certain that Lady Wilcox was in a state of shock. Upon consideration, I doubt she will treat you harshly."

Holmes strode again out into the hallway, motioning us to follow. When he reached the stairs, he pulled out his magnifying glass, and began to examine them carefully, one step at a time, until he was halfway to the bedrooms.

"The bedrooms," he called back. "Who sleeps where, if I might ask?"

"The servants' quarters are off to the right, sir," Davis replied. "Sir Arthur and Her Ladyship occupy the chambers to the left."

"Then their bedrooms are directly above the study."

"Yes, sir."

"And were the hall lamps lit at the time you discovered Sir Arthur's body?"

"No, sir. Only the one at the bottom of the staircase, near the bell cord. Sir Arthur was in the habit of extinguishing that himself, when he retired."

"Ah, then that explains it."

"Explains what, sir?" the butler inquired.

"Why Lady Wilcox brought a candle as she rushed downstairs."

"Oh, but she didn't, sir. She had no candle. Of that, I am quite sure."

Holmes bent down and scraped loose some pieces of white-coloured material from the banister, which he examined closely with his magnifying glass.

"Then who did? These last three posts are clearly spotted

with wax. The drops, you will note if you rub them between your fingers, are most decidedly fresh."

"Then that means someone else was on the stairs," I suggested.

Once again, Holmes demurred.

"Now just a minute," Lestrade expostulated. "Are you trying to tell me that the killer, instead of entering by the front door, made his way down these stairs?"

"I am inferring nothing of the sort," Sherlock Holmes replied, "but I am beginning to see light."

Holmes replaced his magnifying glass in his coat pocket, a pensive look upon his aquiline face. From past experience, I realised that his brilliant mind had already raced far ahead, proffering and then discarding one possible explanation after another, and as I saw him standing there, transfixed, I knew he had found the one solution that fitted.

"The question," he murmured, "is not only who came down these stairs, but why? Although I feel certain of my theory, that is the point that still eludes me." Suddenly, he looked as if stunned. "Of course," he said. "It was not what was upon the desk, but what was not!"

Back into the study he raced, with all of us in tow.

"See there," he cried, "just to the right of the body. I was a fool to not have noticed it earlier. A paper was there that has been removed."

"And what of it?" Lestrade questioned. "The answer to that is also a quite simple one. The killer obviously forced Sir Arthur to write some sort of addendum to the stolen papers – to verify their authenticity. His handwriting, you must admit, would be as proof as a royal seal."

Lestrade drew a small cigar from the breast pocket of his coat and struck a match, a satisfied look upon his face. It was his habit, I had observed, when he felt certain that he had a case in hand.

"You are not the only one with a sharp eye for things, Mr Holmes," he declared. "I thank you for your assistance, but in this case I shall stick to cold, hard facts." A smug look came upon his face. "That fellow Aristotle you mentioned might knock me for sixes in the classroom, but real police work is another matter entirely. True, there are a few details that still elude me, but you must admit, there is very little here that I have missed."

Holmes threw up his hands.

"Alas," he cried, in some despair, "I fear that you have missed everything!"

He swung around to the butler.

"Tell me now, Davis," he asked pointedly, "did you remove anything from this desk?"

"No, sir, I swear," the big man answered.

"Then," Holmes said, "it must still be somewhere close at hand ..."

Dropping to his knees, he looked beneath the ornate desk, reaching desperately underneath.

"Ah!" he cried suddenly, "I have found it. It is here."

He handed Lestrade a small sheet of yellow paper, which had been folded in half. On it was written a brief message:

> *In the garden.*
> *Bring the money.*
> *An hour past midnight.*

Lestrade groaned.

"Good Lord!" he exclaimed. "This proves that there has been treachery here. The selling of secrets, scandal and blackmail. Why, I could never have believed it of Sir Arthur."

Holmes was remarkably unflustered.

"Pray calm yourself," he told the Inspector gravely. "This note merely confirms what I suspected. There has been no diplomatic thievery here. No compromise upon the throne. I can assure you, there is only one victim in all of this ... " He glanced down at Wilcox, still across his desk. "One righteous man who, sad to say, is now beyond our power to assist."

"Sir Arthur?" the policeman gasped.

Holmes nodded.

At that instant, I could not be sure who was more astonished – Lestrade, or I. Yet, in spite of my surprise, I immediately felt certain that it was Holmes, rather than the police, who was on the right track.

"I cannot imagine how I could have missed it," Holmes said, motioning at the desk. "There are bloodstains everywhere – save for that particular spot. Ergo, something must have been there. Something that is not there now. Note the size, Lestrade. It is just right for a sheet of foolscap."

"Your finding does not change my basic theory," Lestrade insisted, though I noted with some hesitation. "As I said before, I believe the killer forced Sir Arthur to write some sort of verification."

"Sir Arthur, I am convinced, did write a final communication before he died," Holmes said. "However, it was not of that nature." He frowned. "That letter is what I seek. It will, I am certain, explain all. What you hold, Lestrade, was the missive that caused it to be written."

Lestrade suddenly gave Holmes a withering look.

"I see where you are coming from," he said, almost derisively. There was anger in his voice as he continued. "Are you saying that a man of Sir Arthur's reputation took his own life, and that this death was a suicide?"

"I am," Holmes said.

"But that cannot be ... "

"It is and I shall prove it," Holmes responded. "In fact, I shall stake my reputation upon it. A man dies of a gunshot wound in his own study. Forget who that man is for the moment, but realise that no one could have entered, or left, from the terrace. Realise that entering by the front door is a far-fetched possibility. Realise that someone did traverse that staircase not once – but twice. I think now what really happened here should quickly come to mind."

"You mention everything but the most important point," Lestrade stated. "What is the motive for Sir Arthur to end his own life?"

"On that, I cannot yet be certain," Holmes admitted, "but I imagine Mr Davis can be of some help to us regarding this matter." He drew the butler within his steely gaze. "Tell me now without delay for the truth is more important than any loyalty to your employer. Had Sir Arthur been overly distressed of late?"

Davis hesitated before heaving a sigh.

"He had seemed on edge for quite some time," the man admitted. "More so, I'd say, in recent weeks. As I mentioned earlier, I put it down to his increased duties – and this incessant heat. Only once did I dare broach the subject, and he refused to speak."

"Did he receive any messages today?"

"Yes, sir, one. It was delivered around half past five."

"You took it to him?"

"Yes, sir. Sir Arthur was in the study, reading *The Times* on the *chaise longue*."

"And what was his reaction when he opened it? Were you able to see?"

Davis sighed heavily again.

"His face turned ashen, sir. I could tell, by his manner, that he was quite upset. I inquired if there was a problem, and if there was any help that I might render. He looked at me, almost fondly I do believe, said that there wasn't, and so I left the room."

Holmes thrust the small sheet of yellow notepaper before the butler's face.

"Could this have been that message?" he asked.

"It could have been, sir," Davis answered. "It is about the right size, as I recall, and the paper is the same colour as well."

Holmes gave Davis a long, inquisitive look.

"But this is not, I take it, the first such message – of this type and colour – that your master has received?"

Davis nodded.

"You are correct, sir," he said. "There have been others. Normally delivered on the first Friday of every month, and always at about five-thirty in the afternoon."

"And for how long?"

Davis thought a moment.

"For months, sir," the butler answered. "The first arrived in April, as I recall."

Holmes smiled.

"It was a time, no doubt, when Sir Arthur was normally at home. Furthermore, the days, I'll wager, correspond exactly to many of the nights he chose to – how did you phrase it – retire late?"

"Yes, sir," Davis confirmed. "And I hated every day that they arrived, because it always put my master in a fury."

"One other point, Mr Davis. Your wife ..."

"Yes, sir?"

"You are certain she has been at Lady Wilcox's side since you took her to her room?"

"To the best of my knowledge, sir. She was at her side when I fetched the maid and sent for Doctor Morrison, and I know all three were there when Doctor Morrison was admitted."

Holmes' gimlet eyes gleamed with anticipation.

"Excellent," he cried. "Then the answer to our puzzle should still be within our grasp. We need only to employ a simple ruse in order to secure it."

"Ruse?" Lestrade questioned. Before continuing he drew close, lowering his voice so that only Holmes and I should hear. "I know you have your ways, Mr Holmes," he admitted, "but this is a very serious matter. Sir Arthur was a personal friend of Lord Salisbury. Despite what you say, the repercussions of all this could be enormous. I'll not allow you any tomfoolery."

Holmes eyed the policeman coldly.

"Very well, Lestrade," he said, with a hint of scorn, "since you no longer seem to have need of our assistance, we shall return to our lodgings. The hour is late, and we are here only at your request." He paused a moment, then added, "this is a delicate matter, and we are presently at the Rubicon. You have two choices: Follow my lead – which you have oft found profitable in the past – or stand firm by your theory. Should you decide on the latter, I daresay, you might never solve this crime. There will be no feather in your cap this time around."

Lestrade fumed, stung to the quick. Yet it was clear by his

look that he did not relish proceeding without my companion's assistance – especially now that the threads of his theory had begun to unravel. For some time, he stewed silently in the juices of his own ineptitude while he pondered a suitable reply.

Decision was temporarily spared the Inspector by a loud knock upon the study door – after which, a well-dressed man with resolute bearing was admitted by the constable on guard. His one hand held a top hat and stick, the other the small black bag so familiar to my profession.

"I am Doctor Morrison," he declared, as he approached us. "The officer requested I speak to an Inspector Lestrade before I departed, presumably as to the condition of Lady Wilcox."

"You are correct," Lestrade told the man. "I should like to know if you feel that she is able to answer a few questions. Oh, and these are Mr Sherlock Holmes and Doctor Watson." He paused. "They are assisting me in this investigation."

Catching Holmes' eye I suppressed a smile. Lestrade, it seemed, had made his decision after all.

"I have heard of your reputation, sir," the doctor said to Holmes. "I can only pray that you are able to bring this foul killer to justice." He turned to Lestrade. "As to any questions, they shall have to wait. Her Ladyship's condition, I must tell you, is extremely unstable. Any further distress tonight could lead to serious consequences. What she needs now is rest."

"There is one thing that I must know," Holmes asked the man. "Are the cook and maid still at her bedside?"

"Why, yes, I have instructed them to remain there, in shifts, throughout the night. I have also left a dram upon Her Ladyship's nightstand, in case she changes her mind."

Holmes appeared relieved.

"Ah, she refused a sedative, then?"

Morrison nodded.

"I could not convince her otherwise," he admitted, "in spite of the fact that her nerves are clearly in a heightened state. As I said, the last thing she needs at this time is further distress."

"And that is why you refused her request?"

Morrison appeared struck.

"However did you know of that?" he asked incredulous. "Are you a clairvoyant, Mr Holmes, or were you merely listening outside the bedroom door?"

Holmes smiled thinly.

"I am not a medium, nor a busybody, sir," he explained. "You must realise you were not the first to have heard her plea."

"Whatever do you mean?"

"It is a natural enough one, I suppose. Granting her a moment or two alone with the deceased to say farewell."

Morrison glanced over at the desk, where Wilcox's body lay.

"And yet, you must agree," he insisted, "that to see him in that condition would certainly do more harm than good. Later, at the mortuary, perhaps."

Holmes gave Lestrade a knowing look.

"I quite think otherwise, Doctor," he told the physician. "You must grant her wish, if the truth of this matter is to see light."

Morrison's eyes widened.

"Are you inferring that Lady Wilcox is somehow involved in this matter?" he asked coldly.

"I am," Holmes replied. "Do as I say, and she herself will tell us to what degree."

Anger flooded the doctor's face, and his eyes became as if

of steel, as he glared at Holmes.

"Shame, sir!" he cried. "Show me your proof at once, or I shall consider you guilty of slander."

It was clear things were at an *impasse*. Yet it was, at that strained moment, that Lestrade's tenacity saved the day.

"I would hold on a moment, Doctor," he said, with some authority. "This is a police matter, you know. I have been given specific instructions by the Foreign Office, and Mr Holmes and I are answerable only to Whitehall in this affair. I suggest you do exactly as Mr Holmes requests."

"And if I refuse?"

Lestrade pointed his cigar at Morrision as if it were a gun.

"Then I shall have no choice but to arrest you for the obstruction of justice," he declared, "and send Doctor Watson instead."

Morrison's recalcitrance wilted before Lestrade's verbal broadside. Silently he shrugged.

"Then you present me with a *fait accompli*," he decided. "I shall acquiesce to your request, but I am placing responsibility for Her Ladyship's health in Doctor Watson's hands."

"A fair enough request," I agreed. "If there is a risk, I feel, it is taken in a good cause."

"Very well, then. What are your instructions, Mr Holmes?"

"Inform Her Ladyship that there has been a delay in reaching Inspector Lestrade, but that you have convinced Sergeant Potter – for whatever reason – that she should be allowed a few moments with Sir Arthur. Bring her directly from her bed to the study – let her venture nowhere else – then wait outside until I call. I pray, not a word of our presence here. Not if you wish the truth."

Morrison, it was clear, was not at all pleased, as without a word he left the room.

"Pardon me, if I am a little puzzled," Lestrade remarked, once the door had closed, "but what are we trying to accomplish?" He eyed Holmes directly. "I have a stake in this, too, you know. I deserve an explanation."

"All in good time," Holmes assured him. "Hurry now! We must take our positions. Lestrade, join the constable on the terrace, if you please. Remember, not a sound until you hear my voice. Potter, you and Davis join the others in the hall – but not a word when Lady Wilcox descends. Stand some distance away, and act as if you are questioning him. It is crucial that nothing arouses her suspicions."

THREE

I have to admit that I too was puzzled by all of this. That Holmes was laying some sort of trap for Lady Wilcox was clear enough – but I could not fathom why. If Sir Arthur's death was indeed a suicide, what had we to gain? Further as a medical man, I did have some reservations about submitting the woman to the grisly scene.

My thoughts were interrupted by Holmes' hand upon my arm.

"Here, Watson," he motioned, "we shall crouch down behind the settee."

Moving quickly about the room, Holmes turned down all but the reading lamps upon the desk, leaving the room in deepest shadow, before returning to my side. I decided to risk one last inquiry.

"This is a bit irregular, you must admit," I whispered.

Holmes smiled faintly.

"So was our sojourn to Briony Lodge[6]," he replied, "but it

---

[6] A Scandal in Bohemia

produced the desired effect." He put a finger to his lips. "No more words now, Watson. She should be here any second."

As we crouched thus in darkness, my brain was flooded with a sense of *déjà vu*. How often during our years together, had Holmes and I waited thus in order to catch a criminal and see a case through to its conclusion. Our chilling vigil at Stoke Moran[7], and our long cold stay outside Manor House in Birlstone[8], immediately came to mind. And now, here we were, waiting in the shadows once again. In this case, however, I felt reasonably certain that the climax was close at hand. What baffled me was the implied involvement of Lady Wilcox, and what Holmes was maybe anticipating. That Sir Arthur was being blackmailed seemed clear. But by whom, and for what reasons? When it came to matters of State, I could not believe he had ever acted dishonourably. Was the cause more close to home I wondered? Davis, it seemed, was not telling all he knew. His story of locked, and unlocked, doors had not set well with me. Had he secretly harboured a grudge against his employer? Might the blackmail notes simply have come from him all along? If so, was his wife an accomplice, providing a timely alibi and assistance? What about the maids – even those of the highest circles, I knew, were not immune to affairs of the heart with their employers? My mind was awhirl with questions. While I sensed a vague outline of the puzzle, I could not bring the pieces home to fit a theory. Holmes, quite obviously, had observed much that I had missed – and summarily deduced far more than I could imagine. Looking back now, I realise there was no way I could have anticipated what would happen – or that this

---

[7] The Speckled Band

[8] The Valley of Fear

would be but the first of two tense watches we would undertake on this steamy summer night, before a conclusion was finally reached.

My reverie was suddenly interrupted by the soft click of the latch as the study door swung open. If Holmes was correct, the solution to our problem was at hand. I felt my pulse quicken.

For a moment, the silhouette of a woman in nightclothes was outlined in the doorway, although the light from the outer hall was not sufficient to reveal her face. Quickly, she closed the door behind her – and for a few suspenseful seconds, the only sound within the darkened room was the soft swishing of her skirts upon the carpet, as she made her way to her husband's side.

As she bent over Sir Arthur's body, her countenance was revealed in the soft glow of the desk lamps. Seldom had I seen a more disconsolate face. Her eyes were red and swollen, her cheeks pale and drawn, and the long tresses of her greying hair hung dishevelled about her shoulders. Her look, I felt, was one of complete despair. Medical experience had trained me to expect stifled sobs, or words of grief at moments such as these. What I saw instead, startled me to the quick.

Without a word, the woman lifted her husband's ink-soaked sleeve, felt beneath it, and then returned it carefully to its place. In a trice, she began to hurriedly search all about the top of the desk, moving the book and glasses, the letterbox, even the scattered sheets of foolscap.

Dropping to her knees, just as Holmes had done, she repeatedly peered and reached beneath the desk, then rose again to her feet.

"Oh, Lord," she murmured with dismay, "where can it be?"

At that instant Holmes sprang up from behind the couch.

"I have the note, Lady Wilcox!" he cried, holding the yellow scrap before him. "It is Sir Arthur's final letter – which you have in your possession – that I desire to see."

With a startled cry of anguish, the woman instinctively clutched at the pocket of her nightdress, then swayed, and collapsed in a heap upon the floor.

"Good Lord, Holmes!" I exclaimed. "She has fainted. Bring up the lights – and fetch the brandy."

"Now, Lestrade!" Holmes cried.

In an instant, Holmes and I were at the woman's side. As I tended to her, pandemonium reigned about me, as Lestrade did as he was instructed – and the others, led by Morrison and Davis, charged in.

"You scoundrel!" Morrison shouted at Holmes. "You will suffer for this!"

"Not now," I counselled him. "Help me get Her Ladyship to the settee."

Between us, we did our best to make Lady Wilcox comfortable, gently raising her head upon the pillows, and loosening her clothing. Davis, able man he was, was at our side immediately, proffering a glass of his master's best brandy. That, along with a whiff or two of ammonia from Morrison's bag, was enough to bring Lady Wilcox round. Gratefully, she accepted a sip of the liquid that I offered.

"You will forgive me, Lestrade," Holmes said, "but you know I can never resist a touch of the dramatic." Steadily, he returned Morrison's angry glance. "Besides, it was our only chance of securing this ..."

From his pocket, Holmes withdrew a folded sheet of foolscap, which I immediately recognised as identical to those on Sir Arthur's desk. As Holmes opened the sheet, I noted that it was splattered with flecks of blood.

"And what is that?" Lestrade cried, moving to my companion's side.

"It is a letter written by Sir Arthur Wilcox, moments before he died," Holmes stated. He glanced down at the forlorn woman. "It is also the letter I retrieved from Her Ladyship's pocket after her collapse. A letter, I might add, that Lady Wilcox did not intend for any of us should see."

Lestrade frowned with consternation. The implications of Holmes' remarks were clear, but given the prominence of the people involved, he was hesitant – at least at this moment – to burst forth with accusations of any kind.

Quickly, he pulled Holmes aside.

"Are you suggesting she killed her husband?" he asked, his voice nothing more than a whisper.

Holmes shook his head.

"It is as I ventured earlier, Lestrade," he replied. "Sir Arthur's death was indeed a suicide. This note only confirms it." He cast his gaze upon the woman before him. "Am I not right, madam?"

With hate brimming from her eyes, Lady Althea Wilcox raised herself to a sitting position upon the couch.

"You are, it seems, a clever man," she told my friend coldly. "But who, sir, are you to make such an accusation?"

"I am Sherlock Holmes, Lady Wilcox," he informed her with equal coolness, "and this is Inspector Lestrade of Scotland Yard. The Foreign Office has retained us to insure that justice is done in this unfortunate affair."

The woman snorted her contempt.

"There is no justice," she declared spitting out the words, "or else you would not have discovered that letter – and there would have been no reason for its writing."

Holmes said nothing, but passed Sir Arthur's last communication to Lestrade who read it out aloud once everybody save myself, Holmes, Morrison and Lady Wilcox had departed.

My Dearest Althea,

These payments, as you well know, cannot continue. Yet, if I refuse, I will surely be exposed, and bring dishonour upon us both. My one alternative is clear. Ahead lies sure disgrace and ruin. Through my folly, I have compromised not only our marriage, but my position of responsibility in the Government as well. This has, as you know, weighed heavily upon my mind these past months. A man's reputation is all that he truly possesses, and I have thrown mine to the winds. There is nothing more to say. Except to ask your forgiveness for the hurt that I have brought upon you.

Love as before all this,

Arthur

For a moment, none of us spoke.

"It has often been said," I remarked sombrely, "that justice is in the eye of the beholder."

"Justice!" the woman scoffed. "What justice was there for me is this? I have been a loyal wife. I stood by him long after others would have left. My only crime, sir, was to try and keep scandal from our door – in spite of his unfortunate weakness."

"For that," Holmes said softly, "you have our deepest sympathy. We are not here to torment you, madam. This is a sad affair, and your actions – at least to me – are quite understandable. Make no mistake, I am well aware of what transpired here tonight, and to the degree to which you are involved. My only question is why did you attempt to make it appear that a robbery had taken place?"

Lady Wilcox took another sip of brandy, but said nothing.

"You think I exaggerate?" Holmes asked. "Very well, I shall quickly set things straight. You knew for quite some time that your husband was being blackmailed, that he was in a position where he could no longer afford to pay, and that a scandal of great proportion was imminent if he did not. He is a honourable man, in most respects at least, and you had worried for some time that this might be the path he chose. Hence, you could not sleep soundly until Sir Arthur had retired upon those nights he chose to stay up late.

"And tonight, your worst fears came to pass. It happened. You heard the shot, lit a candle, rushed downstairs, and found him at his desk. You locked the study doors, rifled through the papers in his safe, and placed the gun where we now see it. It was then, I imagine, that Davis happened to inquire – sending you into a panic. You grabbed the damning note and letter – or so you thought – and once you were sure that Davis had left, you hurried back up to your bedroom.

117

"Your intent, of course, was to destroy them both – but you did not have the note. Realising that in your haste, you had dropped it, you had no choice but to return. But there was Davis blocking your path to the study. Your attempts to bluff him failed, and you were returned to your room. Worse yet, there was no chance to destroy Sir Arthur's letter – for always there was someone at your side. Naturally, you refused any medication or drink, since you still hoped to recover the note … "

"Enough!" Lady Wilcox cried. "It is clear that you know all." She eyed Holmes warily, before continuing. "This must all be kept secret, you understand? In the best interests of the Government it must – I beg you."

"And, most assuredly, in yours as well," Holmes added dryly.

Indignation flashed in the woman's grey eyes.

"Whatever do you mean?" she demanded.

"The money is almost gone, is it not?" Holmes inquired. "I suspect there is little left." Lady Wilcox began to protest, but he waved her to silence. "I have no doubt, madam, that your husband was heavily insured," Holmes stated, "and since you are the daughter of Edward Balmaster, who owns the largest agency in London, I am certain you would know that no insurer in this city would pay upon a suicide."

Slowly, the woman put down her glass. A dull tiredness reflected in her eyes, and her lined face was a mask of sadness. Her last reserves, I felt, had been spent. She looked up at Holmes with resignation

"There was a woman," she said, her low voice as hollow as a reed. "She was a one-time actress, I am told, by the name of Helen Millay. How Arthur met her, I have no idea. But he did meet her, in July of last year. The change in his nocturnal habits was immediately noticeable. He began dining at his club more often, and some nights he did not return until after midnight. I questioned him, of course, but he denied everything. It was two nights after that confrontation that I first heard him say her name in his sleep."

She reached for her glass, and took another sip.

"You cannot imagine the deadening sense of betrayal to which I succumbed. We had celebrated our thirty-second wedding anniversary that June. Not once, in all those years, had Arthur given me the slightest cause to doubt him. Still, I felt I needed to be certain. And so, when I was next informed that he would return late, I hired a hansom – and waited in the darkness outside the Foreign Office until he appeared.

"At precisely eight-thirty, I observed my husband leave the building and hail a cab. God knows, gentlemen, I prayed that he would lead me west back to the house, or to be deposited at St. James' on Piccadilly. Instead, I followed him north for nearly a half hour, until he alighted before a building overlooking Regent's Park. You can imagine my shock and outrage, when I saw him greeted at the door by a tall young woman with curled blonde hair." Again she reached for her glass. "For half an hour I waited, fighting back the tears, my mind all but numbed with pain. Finally, I told the driver to take me home, if that was what you could call it anymore ... "

"Gentlemen," Morrison interrupted, "I do think this is enough. How cold of heart can you be? This woman has suffered terribly. You know now, it seems to me, more than enough to conclude your investigation. I must insist that you refrain from this interrogation and allow Her Ladyship the rest she sorely needs."

To my surprise Lady Wilcox waved him silent.

"No, William," she said firmly, "it is better I get through

119

this now." She gave him a look of fondness, and a slight smile. "You have been a trusted friend these last few months. Please know that your steadfast protection of my health – and feelings – is something I shall not forget."

Turning back to us she continued with incredible strength and frankness.

"You must realise that all romance between us died that night," she said. "That Arthur cared for another, I forced myself to accept. I realised that I had my own position – and future – to consider. I consulted my father upon the matter – swearing him to silence – and received advice concerning financial matters, as I felt I must look out for my own well-being.

"Upon my father's advice I also hired a private detective in order to document my husband's indiscretions. I must admit he was most efficient. Within a month, he had supplied me with the woman's name, her last known stage appearance, and her theatrical history. Why, can you believe it? She had performed in musicals at both *The Lyceum* and at *The Strand* ..." The woman's face stiffened. "I was also horrified to learn, that in addition to the apartment, my husband was providing her with considerable support – including a carriage and a private box at the opera.

"At that point, I could withhold myself no longer. The next time Arthur arrived home late – smelling of a perfume I had come to recognise – I confronted him with all that I had learned and demanded an explanation, else he should leave the house at once."

"And his reaction?" Holmes asked.

The woman sighed.

"Oh, he was quite contrite," she told us coldly. "He pleaded with me to forgive him, but I informed him that was out of the question. Naturally, there were our reputations to consider. For that reason – and that reason only – I agreed to remain. But only if he never saw Helen Millay – or any other woman – again." She paused for a moment, then added, "that was the week before Christmas last."

"And when, to your knowledge, did the first note arrive?" Holmes asked.

"In the spring, a few months before Lord Salisbury took office," Lady Wilcox answered. "My husband was so terrified he actually showed it to me. In return for her silence, she demanded a sum of ten thousand pounds."

"Which he paid?"

"Which he paid – despite my objections. I implored him to speak first with the Prime Minister. I am sure you know how that works, Mr Holmes. Pressure can be applied. Alibis can be arranged. I felt certain that with some official assistance the harlot's claims could be easily refuted."

"But your husband did not do so?"

"No. He paled at the thought of Lord Salisbury knowing."

Holmes noticed something in her face.

"And ..."

"There were also letters," she admitted. "Letters written on my husband's personal stationary."

Holmes whistled.

"Ah, but stationary can be stolen, can it not? Surely, a claim of forgery could have been made."

Lady Wilcox shook her head sadly.

"If it had only been that simple," she observed with a groan. "She also told him there was a child."

For an instant, we were all too stunned to speak. A stricken look appeared upon Holmes' face.

"I see," he murmured. "And so, month by month, the

payments continued."

Lady Wilcox nodded in silent assent.

"My private detective attempted to discover if the claim was true," she explained, "but he was without success. The woman had left the apartment in Regent's Park some time before, and he was unable to locate her present dwelling."

Holmes began to pace back and forth, as he thought.

"Such a disappearance is easy to understand," he concurred. "For an actress, the change would be a simple matter. An alias, a wig, or change of hairstyle would certainly suffice. Given the financial resources your husband had already provided, a residence in almost any location would be within her reach." Holmes paused. "These notes – did they arrive by post, or were they hand-delivered? A postmark would tell us much."

"All were hand delivered and, to my recollection, no messenger was ever the same."

Holmes frowned.

"How unfortunate," he remarked, "but pray continue, Lady Wilcox. Surely, there has occurred an incident that brought all these matters to a head."

"You are correct of course. It was one week ago, to this very day. Arthur had arrived home a little later than usual, looking pale and very upset. Knowing what I did, I was alarmed and immediately inquired. To my amazement, he threw down his hat and stick, led me into this very room, and locked the doors behind us. As you may imagine, I was incredulous, when he revealed that he had just spoken with Helen Millay!"

Not even Holmes could hide his surprise.

"He met with her, you say, but given his promise and all that had happened, how and why did this meeting occur?"

"Arthur insisted it was not prearranged. Upon leaving the Foreign Office, he had hailed a cab – and was shocked to find her waiting when he climbed inside. There was a man beside her, he told me, with a pistol in his hand."

"It is a common trick," Lestrade remarked. "No doubt, they had waited for your husband for quite some time. Both the ruffian and driver, I'll wager, were in her employ."

"And what of Helen Millay?" Holmes inquired intently. "How did your husband describe her? Did she appear to be with child?"

"Unfortunately, there is nothing to say," she said. "My husband said she wore a veil that concealed her face from view, though he recognised her voice, of course. At any rate, the discussion lasted only minutes, and then he was deposited at Montague House, while they fled north towards Charing Cross. As to your last point she did wear clothes which made her seem pregnant but as an actress she could easily have arranged to appear as such."

Holmes gave the woman a knowing look.

"And how much did she ask for this time?" he questioned.

"More than we could afford," Lady Wilcox replied. "Another twenty thousand pounds, to be exact. In exchange for the sum, Arthur would receive the letters he had sent her and never hear from her again. She planned to sail for America it seems."

"And if he refused?"

"Then the letters, along with full details of the scandal, would be given to the highest bidder on Fleet Street – on the morning before he departed for the Continent."

"That would be Monday, two days from now," I interjected. "So the note he received today was quite likely a final demand."

"I suspect so," Lady Wilcox agreed.

"And yet, on this occasion," Holmes interjected, "Sir Arthur decided not to pay. Could he not somehow have secured the needed funds, and been finally rid of this pestilence?"

She gave Holmes a baleful glance.

"Only by confiding in my father," she replied, "and that he would never do. His pride would not allow from him a loan or gift of any kind. Nor would he approach any other agency, for fear of public discovery. The political consequences of a scandal at this time, he felt, would be immense – and certainly damaging to the Prime Minister. It was not a risk he was prepared to take."

Holmes, I could see, was clearly affected by her words.

"A tangled skein, to be sure," he murmured. "How ironic, for it seems his final act will most surely bring about the scandal he did so hope to avoid."

Lestrade produced a match, and relit his cigar – a satisfied look upon his face.

"I think that I have heard enough," he concluded. "This has been a tragic affair, but it has all become clear as crystal, now that Mr Holmes and I have put things into their proper order." He turned to Lady Wilcox. "You may retire now, madam. As a policeman, you must realise that I cannot condone your actions. They must be included in my official report. However, given your assistance, I doubt any charges will be placed. However, I must have your word that, for the time being, you will not leave this house without my permission."

"You have it," Lady Wilcox replied. "I only ask that you understand my motives, and the torment with which I have lived these recent months, wondering what was to become of us. I can only compare it to standing at the edge of a giant abyss, knowing that unless a miracle occurred, you someday must fall in."

Lady Wilcox rose to her feet, and glanced over at the body of her dead husband, sprawled across his desk.

"He ground all the love out of me, you know," she said speaking to no one in particular. "Oh, there was the initial shock of finding him – but I must admit, the tears I have shed tonight were mostly for myself." She strode over to Doctor Morrison's side. "I am relieved that this is over," she told him. "Your sedative, I hope, will provide me with the respite I sorely need."

"I am certain that it will," he assured her. He turned to Holmes in angry displeasure. "And good night to you, sir," he stated severely. "You have discerned the truth in this affair, I will give you that, but as a physician, I cannot approve of your methods."

My friend gave Morrison a look of scorn.

"As a physician," he retorted, "it is not within your realm to do so. Your approval, or lack of it, matters little to me. What matters is that the truth has finally come to light, and that the integrity of the Government remains secure."

Morrison's face darkened with anger. For a moment, he glared fiercely at us all, then took Lady Wilcox by the arm and escorted her from the room. No sooner had they left, than Sergeant Potter entered the room, followed by a rumpled looking fellow I took to be the coroner, two constables with a trolley, and Davis.

"All finished, Inspector?" the fellow asked as he approached us.

"Quite so, Ormsby," Lestrade informed him briskly. "You may remove the body at your discretion. Your report, I trust, will find its way to me by morning."

Holmes quickly checked his watch, as the coroner began to turn away.

"How long will your duties take you?" he asked pointedly. "If more than a few minutes, I would ask that you wait ... "

"I must examine the body, and take my notes," the coroner stated. "Only then can we be off. A half an hour, at least."

"Then, indeed, I insist you have a seat," Holmes told him. "For while our investigation is complete, there are still important matters that are ripe."

He looked at his watch again as if for confirmation.

"An hour after midnight, remember? And it is now twelve-thirty. If we are fortunate, we may still nab our bird of prey this very night."

Lestrade frowned.

"Not her," he concluded, "she is too clever. My guess is she will send an accomplice here instead."

Holmes shook his head.

"Not with twenty thousand pounds at stake," he insisted with a wave. "Oh, she may be accompanied by a ruffian – it would seem to be her style, but, mark my words, she will want that money placed in her own hands."

A sly look crossed Lestrade's ferret-like face. He was, imagined, already visioning the triumph that such a capture would bring.

"If that is the case, we shall have her then!" he exclaimed. "I am at your disposal, Mr Holmes ..."

"Then hurry as there are only moments to spare. Place your men discreetly in the bushes, and remove all vehicles from the drive. Anyone not involved in our vigil should remain here and silent. Watson, take some envelopes from the desk, and stuff them full of foolscap."

"Of course, Holmes."

Holmes joined me at the desk, and picked up Sir Arthur's glasses. He turned to Davis.

"Did your master use these only for reading?"

"Yes, sir. He preferred a pince-nez in public."

"Be so good as to fetch them then along with one of Sir Arthur's jackets, his stick, and a bowl of flour from the kitchen."

"Right away, sir."

Lestrade eyed Holmes incredulously.

"And why do you want these items?" he demanded.

Holmes looked at the dour Inspector with some amusement.

"I am asking for your indulgence a second time this evening," he replied. "One act remains to be played in this affair – and it is about to be played by me."

FOUR

M inutes later, our second vigil of the night was underway. This time, I was concealed – as was Lestrade and two of his men – behind the bushy evergreens that encircled the moonlit garden on either side of the terrace. Before us was a small fishpond with a gushing fountain at its centre, surrounded by cobblestone paths and flowers all around. Stone benches with lion motifs graced the area, and it was there – upon the closest bench to our right – that Sherlock Holmes now sat. Behind him, the wide lawn trailed off into the distance, towards tall hedges and a few large plane trees. A breeze, I noticed, had picked up. Might it be a harbinger of cooler weather moving in I wondered?

In all our years together, I had never ceased to be amazed at Holmes' mastery in the art of disguise. One of his earliest roles, as an aged mariner[9], had fooled not only me, but Inspector Athelney Jones of Scotland Yard as well. His long list of impersonations included a drunken groom, a clergyman, a common loafer, even an Italian priest, and how

---

[9] The Sign of Four

could I ever forget his ruse as an elderly deformed bibliophile[10], who I had inadvertently knocked to the ground at No. 427 Park Lane?

At our rooms in Baker Street Holmes kept at his command a wide variety of makeup, costumes and wigs. Tonight, however, with only the most rudimentary of aids and a few moments of preparation, I felt he had outdone himself. For seated in the moonlight, or so it seemed, was the honourable civil servant, Sir Arthur Wilcox, waiting, it appeared, to make what he hoped would be his final payment to the attractive – and cunning – Helen Millay.

For Holmes the transformation from detective to civil servant had been remarkably simple, in spite of his limited resources. Liberal applications of flour had transformed his shiny black hair into cotton grey, and Sir Arthur's jacket, pince-nez and walking stick had made the transition complete.

"I must admit," Lestrade whispered, "he gives me the shudders at times. Why, you would think that was Sir Arthur sitting there."

"We shall hope," I whispered back, "that Helen Millay feels the same."

Anxiously, I peered about the dark edges of the grounds, hoping to catch some sign of movement. Two gates, Davis had told us, opened onto the property from the rear, but all was moonlight and shadow, peaceful and still. Impatiently, I reached for my watch, as the minutes dragged on. Three minutes past one. Had something gone amiss I wondered with our quarry somehow sensing a trap and fleeing?

A heartbeat later my question was answered when I saw

---

[10] The Empty House

two men approaching silently across the lawn. One was plump, of medium height, and who walked with quick graceful steps. The other was a good six feet tall, I calculated – and solid. What caught my attention as they advanced towards us in the moonlight was the gleaming shape of a revolver in the larger man's right hand. Instinctively, Lestrade and I exchanged glances; he produced a weapon as well. Silently, I rued the fact that I had taken Holmes' earlier advice, and could not do the same.

As the pair closed in, Holmes raised his head ever so slightly. At a signal from his companion, the larger fellow halted about twenty feet away, waiting with gun in hand while the other continued on until he had reached my companion's side.

"Quite a risk, isn't it, sitting in the moonlight?" the fellow said. "I expected you at the rear gate. Ah, but I see you have the money."

I was stunned. It was a woman's voice!

Immediately, Holmes rose to his feet, removed the pince-nez, and jauntily tapped the cobblestone walk with his stick.

"A chance, indeed!" he cried. "And yet, well worth it, you must admit. How better to insure meeting such a clever fellow thespian as yourself, face to face?"

Startled by his words, a look of alarm showed upon the woman's face. Warily, she glanced about.

"And who are you?" she asked.

"I am Sherlock Holmes," my friend informed her, "and you, unless I am greatly mistaken, are the viper Helen Millay – whose evil bite has caused this night the death of Sir Arthur Wilcox."

"No ... "

"But, yes, because of your repeated torments, he died by

his own hand, not three hours ago … "

"This is a trick!" she cried.

"A trick of sorts," Holmes told her harshly. "It is the final trick of your sordid game, and it is mine to play. There shall be no more payments, nor any escape for you, or your friend."

As quick as a cat, the woman turned and ran. Shrill blasts of police whistles sounded, as Holmes immediately gave chase. To my horror, as he did, the larger man raised his revolver to fire – but Lestrade, thank God, was a heartbeat quicker. His gun barked once in the night, causing the other to drop his weapon as he fell to the ground, holding his shoulder in pain.

As we rushed out of our hiding places, I caught sight of Holmes racing across the lawn – only a step or two behind the woman ahead. An instant later, we heard her cry out, as Holmes, with a final lunge, grabbed her by the coat sleeve and pulled her to the ground.

"Take charge of him!" Lestrade thundered to a constable, as we ran past the fallen man. Seconds later, we were at Holmes' side, as he was pulling Helen Millay to her feet. Her loose cloth cap, I noticed, had fallen off in the struggle, and her mid-length auburn tresses had now replaced the blonde.

"Congratulations, Lestrade!" Holmes cried in triumph, as he held the woman firmly. "Your bag, I believe, is now complete. I present to you the elusive Helen Millay, whose feline treachery lies at the heart of this matter." Holmes handed the Inspector a small packet. "And these, I imagine are Sir Arthur's letters. The other," he added casting a glance at the wounded ruffian, "is most likely her companion from the cab."

"A splendid job," Lestrade agreed as he clapped the

handcuffs over her wrists. "And what have you to say for yourself, Helen Millay?"

"Nothing, to you," she spat, "but I will have quite a song to sing, if you are foolish enough to bring me to the dock."

"Is that so?" Lestrade replied. "Well, it is my opinion that your trip to America will be delayed, my good woman – by about twenty years, I should say. Blackmail and attempted murder are not slight charges, you know."

"You have no proof," Helen Millay sneered.

"Proof enough," Lestrade stated heatedly. "Thanks to Mr Holmes, every detail of this intrigue has come out. We have these letters, your wounded ruffian and his weapon, and we have you." Lestrade gave her a sarcastic look. "What were you doing here, I might ask? Is it your habit to take nocturnal walks of this sort quite often?"

Helen Millay said nothing, a look of defeat upon her face.

Lestrade motioned to Sergeant Potter, who had arrived at his side.

"Take charge of them both," he told him. "I shall be along to the station directly ... "

"Once there," Holmes interrupted, "you may strip her to clear up one final detail."

The woman gave Holmes an evil look.

"I shall spare myself that indignity," she said. "There never was a child, just padding material that I have taken to wearing for effect."

"I thought as much from the way you ran," my friend commented as Potter took her away.

Lestrade pocketed the damning packet before rubbing his hands together gleefully.

"This has been a baffling matter," he concluded, "but nothing that you and I could not set straight." The Inspector paused, then put out his hand. "You have my thanks, Mr Holmes," he said with an appraising look. "Our methods are quite different I do admit, but between us we have wrapped this matter up quite neatly. I want you to know that down at Scotland Yard you are considered a friend."

"My blushes," Holmes murmured with a smile. "From you, Lestrade, that is high praise indeed."

"Well, I shall be off," the policeman said officiously as we started our walk back to the house. "They will no doubt be wanting my report at Downing Street. Lord only knows what the Prime Minister's reaction will be to what has occurred tonight. Certainly this case was not the scandal they feared – but it is still a scandal of sorts, none the less."

"That, Lestrade, is not our concern," Holmes insisted. "Our duty was to discover the truth, no matter how distasteful that may be. To speculate any further would be to enter the realm of high politics – something I choose not to do. Instead, I shall be content to return with Watson to Baker Street where we shall indulge ourselves in a final pipe and a glass of claret, while I attempt to discern the uniquely cruel depths of feminine design."

I did not press Holmes during the return to our lodgings. However, once we had repaired to our chairs with a glass of wine, I could hold myself back no longer. By any measure, this had been a night of astonishing events – a tragedy of the first magnitude, the final outcome of which we could still only speculate.

"Holmes," I inquired tentatively, "would you mind answering a few questions? There are, I confess, some points about all this I seem to have missed."

"Ask away, Watson. As my Boswell, you are always entitled to know the singular links that make up the deductive chain."

"Very well, then. When we arrived in Belgravia, I saw what you saw, I heard what you heard, and yet, for the life of me, I cannot understand how you realised so quickly what had actually transpired – that Sir Arthur Wilcox had taken his own life."

Holmes chuckled.

"Perhaps that is because I deduced a little more than you," he replied. "Besides, it was the only explanation that fitted. Lestrade's theory, I grant you, had some merit at the beginning – but faced with the facts, it disintegrated rapidly. My suspicions were first aroused by the trajectory of the wound and the location of the gun – which did not match. When we discovered that it was, in fact, Sir Arthur's revolver, and I found no one had traversed the trellis, I knew I was on the right track. The book, however, was the key ..."

"The book? Aristotle's *Nicomachean Ethics* you mean?"

Holmes nodded as he struck a match and lit his pipe.

"That clue was enormous, Watson. Had Sir Arthur been surprised by an intruder it would certainly have been open with his spectacles lying askew, or broken, as he fell when he met his end. That he would have had time to carefully mark the book, remove his glasses and stack both neatly beside him was beyond the realm of possibility.

"The book itself provided me with an invaluable insight as to Sir Arthur's state of mind. *Nicomachean Ethics* is a strict guide on the relationship between injury and justice. When I saw the fourth clause underlined all became clear. It pointed, decidedly to a righteous man in turmoil."

Holmes sent a blue cloud of smoke swirling towards the ceiling.

"How did it go? 'When the act is a result of deliberate

purpose, the doer himself is unjust and wicked'. What other explanation could there be? He had injured someone greatly, Watson, and thereby committed an act that was not pardonable. That person, I reasoned, had to be close to cause such a degree of torment. Who else, then, if not his wife?" My friend took a sip from his glass. "I felt certain then, that Sir Arthur had made a most tragic of choices. All that remained was to determine the reason why."

"But how did you deduce that it was Lady Wilcox who was in the study when Davis called?"

"It was a combination of what she said and what I found. You remember what she told Davis – that she had heard him calling Sir Arthur's name. If that was so, how could she have failed to hear the fatal shot, especially since her bedroom was located directly above the study? There was also the candle wax ..."

"Ah, yes," I concurred sampling my claret.

"Davis said she had no candle, remember? And yet, when I inspected the stairs, there was fresh wax all around. The conclusion was obvious. Lady Wilcox had traversed the stairs not once, but twice."

"But, of course!" I ejaculated. "The first time was when she heard the shot and discovered her husband's body. The second when she attempted to retrieve Helen Millay's message. Knowing Davis might return, she lit no candle for fear of immediate detection."

"Precisely, Watson. It all came together in a flash, as I was standing in the hall. It was then I realised what I should have noted earlier – that we had found no final note from Sir Arthur upon his desk. It was inconceivable that a man of his intellect would quit this world and not leave some explanation behind."

"Thank goodness, then, that Lady Wilcox mislaid the smaller scrap of paper," I commented, "and that she did not have a chance to destroy the other."

"In that, I admit, we were quite fortunate," Holmes admitted. "It was that tiny missive that allowed me to force her hand."

Holmes took another sip from his glass, then closed his eyes, and rested back his head. A faint smile of what I took to be satisfaction was upon his face. If so, I thought, he certainly deserved it. In a short time, that night, he had unravelled a unique enigma that no one else could ever have set straight. By any measure, I decided, he was an amazing person – a superb intellect and yet also a decisive man of action.

As I finished my glass, I could not help but recall Holmes' earlier remarks about the weather and how it affected the frequency of crime. Had the recent weeks of wilting heat helped weaken Sir Arthur's resolution and his resistance to depression? In the final analysis, I concluded, to that I could only guess.

During the early hours of morning, a fierce storm swept through London and out to sea. The cooler, less humid air it brought was indeed a welcome relief from the oppressive summer heat that had, for weeks, held us in its grasp. As was my habit on such rainy mornings, I slept late. When I finally awoke at half past ten, the showers had abated and the skies outside my window were brightening. Only the raindrops that streaked my bedroom window, and the pools of water upon the sill bore evidence to the soaking. Eagerly, I thrust open the window, and was delighted to feel the cool, crisp breeze that greeted me while I made my toilet and dressed.

Holmes, as I suspected, had been up for quite some time. I found him seated in the velvet armchair, already dressed and scanning the morning papers. The windows were thrown open, fresh air billowed through the curtains, and bright sunshine bathed the room. The only disconcerting fact I noted was that blue smoke swirled from his cherry-wood, rather than his clay – a sure signal, I had come to learn, that his mood was not the best.

"Ah, you have finally risen then," he remarked as I entered the room. "No matter, the tea is still hot, and I am certain you will be delighted with breakfast. Mrs Hudson has provided a hearty repast of bacon and eggs."

Holmes gave an angry wave towards the table.

"Now if you care to peruse that copy of *The Telegraph* before you," he said irritably, "its contents, I am sure, will not be to your liking."

Glancing down, I nearly dropped my tea, so startled was I when I saw the glaring headlines which read:

> ## CIVIL SERVANT SLAIN!
>
> ### Police Insist
> ### No Documents
> ### Were Stolen
>
> ---
>
> ### Diamond
> ### Necklace
> ### Missing

"But, Holmes!" I exclaimed. "This is incredible. How ..."

"How, indeed," he remarked angrily. "Were Lestrade here now, I'm certain he could supply all the relevant details. Though, given some thought, what has happened is not too hard to fathom."

"Ah, the Government, you mean ... "

Holmes tossed aside his papers and began to pace about the room in a state of some agitation.

"Who else?" he declared. "I must tell you, however, this was not totally unexpected. I hinted as much to Lestrade last night, as we departed. A remarkable sequence of events has taken place, Watson, while we slept out the storm. A sequence which, I have no doubt, begins with the obsequious Doctor Morrison and ends at the door of the Prime Minister."

"Morrison? Whatever do you mean?"

"It was a tactic I should have foreseen," Holmes explained. "It was obvious by the conversation that his relationship to Lady Wilcox was close. True, she could not leave the grounds, but Lestrade's warning would not have kept Morrison from scurrying off to Downing Street, to present her Ladyship's case."

"Not at all," I agreed as I helped myself to bacon and eggs. "In fact, given his displeasure with us, I feel certain he was a willing ally – willing to throw whatever discredit he could upon ourselves and the police."

Holmes threw himself down at table, began to relight his pipe and then decided against it.

"During the small hours, the decision for subterfuge was made," he stated wearily. "Scotland Yard was given its orders, and the newspapers informed of a horrible murder and robbery that had taken place. In this way Sir Arthur's reputation along with Lady Wilcox's financial position were secured, and an ill-timed scandal was averted. Whoever

139

represents this country in Athens will be received with sympathy, rather than chagrin."

Holmes heaved a sigh, then rose and replaced his cherry-wood upon the shelf, and reached for his familiar black clay. His anger and frustration, I knew, had been spent.

"Ah, well," he said finally, "as you pointed out, Watson, justice is often in the eye of the beholder. There have been times, in the past, when I have taken justice into my hands. This time, although for the common good, it has been taken from me."

"And what of Helen Millay?" I asked. "What will become of her and her accomplice?"

"I suspect that tickets to America have been exchanged for their silence," Holmes ventured. "That, and the threat of prosecution should they ever return. A small enough price to pay, since I'll warrant Millay still has a considerable sum of the blackmail money in her possession."

"But what will happen now with the so-called murder investigation?"

"Weeks will pass," Holmes said with a wave of his hand. "At some point, it will be reported that the necklace has been recovered, though the fugitive is still at large. And that, my dear Doctor, will be that. From the public's standpoint, within a year, the case will be out of sight and out of mind."

"No glory for Lestrade," I said with a wry smile. "I cannot speak for you, Holmes, but my sympathies do not lie with either Lady Wilcox or Helen Millay – in spite of the Government's position."

"Nor do mine," my friend replied, "but it was made clear to me, not an hour ago, that there are others who feel quite differently upon that point."

From his pocket, my friend produced a folded sheet of fine,

white stationary and placed it on table before me. Opening it I gasped as I recognised the official seal.

"Consider it a souvenir for your files," Holmes remarked, "although I doubt this is a case you would ever want to chronicle, for while we solved the crime, to my mind, justice has not been done." He laughed. "Once again, it seems the female sex has outwitted me," he added, "and of course there is Mr Salisbury's reputation to consider. No, I doubt the details of this matter – at least for many years – could ever be made public."

With astonishment I read the letter:

My Dear Sherlock Holmes,

I hope you will accept my personal gratitude for your invaluable assistance given in the unfortunate death of Sir Arthur Wilcox. However, for reasons I cannot divulge, I must ask for your silence in this matter.

There are times, in matters of Government, where perception is as valuable as fact. I believe that if this affair is not properly handled, it could do great harm to our country at a particularly sensitive time.

After speaking with your brother, Mycroft, I feel certain I can count upon your discretion.

It was signed by the Prime Minister.

Sherlock Holmes
and the
Highcliffe Invitation

Eddie Maguire

About the Author

Eddie Maguire was born in 1950 and turned his hand to writing and publishing in the late 1980s after falling prey to the scourge of disability (in body if not mind and spirit). At first he produced a series of five short stories that were later followed by novel length works. Eddie has always been fascinated by the writings of Sir Arthur Conan Doyle and historical research, and it is therefore not surprising to find that certain historical figures feature in his Sherlock Holmes adventures with the greatest care being given to recreating the atmosphere and characters of the era. If proof were needed no less than Freddie Trueman, the noted cricket expert, said of Eddie's *A Death at the Cricket* that 'This story really brings to life the big house cricket matches of the 19th century'.

Eddie is married and lives in Somerset with his wife Mary and their six cats.

By the same author

Sherlock Holmes: The Tandridge Hall Mystery
& other stories

Sherlock Holmes and the Secret Mission

PROLOGUE

In the spring of 1907, Sherlock Holmes retired from practice. As was typical of Holmes, there was no fuss, no ceremony and very little notice given. Oft, he had complained that the London criminal had become a very dull fellow and had it not been for the now celebrated affair of the *Mazarin Stone*, then the months before his retirement would have been little more than a swamp of trifling trivialities.

For myself, I had remarried in 1903, leaving Holmes alone in our rooms at 221B Baker Street and instead of our old Bohemian lifestyle; I now luxuriated in connubial comfort and matrimonial bliss in my new establishment in Barrington Street, West Central.

It was late one afternoon when Holmes called upon me to inform me of his decision. I wondered aloud about Mrs Hudson and her possible reaction to the news. He sighed and ran a long tapering finger down his face.

"That I am also wondering," he replied.

"Then you are set upon bee keeping in Sussex?"

"I am. Indeed, I have only today finalised the transaction. I am ready to take up my residence in a fine cliff-top villa some six or seven miles from Newhaven and not more than a mile or so from the fishing village of Fulworth. It is exactly suited to my needs, Watson."

And so it was that on the first day of July, Sherlock Holmes left Baker Street for the final time. As we parted I made the usual platitudes about how we would see each other from time to time and how the telephone would keep us near to each other, but in my heart of hearts I knew that only a crisis or a matter of considerable gravity would bring us together again in the foreseeable future.

Yet to my great surprise and delight, I only had to wait until October to once again set my eyes upon Holmes. It was a fortuitous moment, for my wife had left me in the temporary care of the housekeeper whilst she paid a long-expected visit upon her sister in Exeter and I have to confess that I was frankly at something of a loose end. Holmes informed me that he was visiting his publisher, and as he had the whole weekend free asked if it would be convenient for him to stay over? I was quick to answer him in the affirmative. Indeed, I almost dragged him bodily into the house in my enthusiasm for the idea. It was then, as we set to discussing the possibilities of visiting the Crystal Palace, or some other site of interest, the whole idea was roughly pushed aside to accommodate a new and exciting offer made by the unexpected arrival of a second and much newer acquaintance.

At first I was rather vexed by the insistent ringing of the doorbell, for with Sherlock Holmes under my roof I was disinclined to waste precious time on others, but when a visitors card was presented to me, it became a wholly different matter, because it turned out to be none other than Colonel, the Honourable Sir Edward Stuart-Wortley.

The Colonel was a splendid fellow whom I had met originally after treating his nephew for a badly broken leg some nine months before. During the intervening period, I had lunched with him at his club in Pall Mall and my wife and I had dined with him and his family at his fine establishment in Belgravia.

Holmes, I was relieved to discover, knew all about the Colonel. In spite of his removal to Sussex, he was still regularly in touch with brother Mycroft and had heard from him of Stuart-Wortley's rise to prominence in the Foreign Office. His eyes lit up at the sight of the Colonels visiting card.

"My word, Watson, tell me my spies do not mislead me; you have gone up in the world during the last few months."

The Colonel appeared in the doorway; he was a tall, rather portly figure in his mid sixties, dressed in the old fashioned style much in favour with the servants of the Crown. He held out a large freckled hand.

"My dear fellow. I was in the district and thought to call upon you and Mrs Watson to ask if you might care to come down to my country place next weekend. I am expecting a particularly august guest of honour whom I know would be delighted to meet you. It will be a jolly affair. What do you say, Watson?"

I explained that although his invitation was most welcome, it came at rather an inopportune moment. My dear wife was presently away and I in fact had a visitor myself. The Colonel turned his eye upon my companion, whom he had clearly not observed until now.

"Why, Mr Holmes; how splendid. So you have extracted yourself from Sussex." He held out his hand. "Old Watson, here has often spoken of you, sir." Then Stuart-Wortley abruptly stopped and stood bowed in thought, his hand placed against his forehead in a most theatrical fashion. "Of course," he cried in a sudden burst of re-animation, "Watson's invitation must be augmented to include yourself. If his wife cannot come, then why not you, sir?"

Holmes gazed in my direction and I gave him an expressive glance intended to indicate my desire to accept the Colonel's offer. Then he smiled his sharp little smile and nodded.

"Of course, my dear Colonel. I should be delighted to accept."

And so it was that we found ourselves boarding a large black motorcar, which the Colonel had sent to take us down to his country retreat in Hampshire. It was mid afternoon when the vehicle arrived and the driver apologised for his lateness, explaining that within moments of leaving the mews where the Colonel's cars were stationed, something had hit the windscreen. He pointed to a small area of grazing in the top right hand corner of the glass. The driver was inclined to believe that a stone thrown up from the tyre of a passing car had done the damage and once he had established that no further harm had been done, he had driven immediately to my address as planned.

It was only later, however, when the driver informed us that as dusk was approaching he would have to stop the car and get the lamps going as he put it, that Holmes was afforded the opportunity of inspecting the damage to the glass more closely. Abruptly he reached into his inside pocket and produced the knife he usually reserved for cleaning the bowl of his pipe, and started poking around in the lining of the cars' roof. Suddenly a small dark object fell into his open hand.

"Here, Watson," he said holding it up for my inspection.

"What do you make of this?"

I took the object from him and scrutinised it carefully.

"Good Lord! This is a flattened bullet, Holmes."

He nodded.

"Indeed; and if I am not very much mistaken it was fired from a powerful air gun."

"An air gun?" I spluttered. "But with what motive?"

"Ah, of that I cannot be certain because too many facts elude me, but judging by its trajectory the bullet was fired not to injure but perhaps to alarm. As for the motive I cannot say."

"We must warn the Colonel," I said.

"That we must."

By the time we reached Highcliffe, darkness had enveloped us completely. The whole atmosphere of the house resembled that of an army, which was on immediate standby for orders to advance, but as yet had failed to receive any. The Colonel greeted us with a strong hand but it was easy to see that his mind was distracted.

"It is my guest of honour," he murmured. "His man telephoned earlier to inform me that His Excellency will be rather late having been delayed by important business. So goodness knows when he will come now."

Clearly with the Colonel so badly upset by the late arrival of his guest, the matter of the soft nose bullet would need to be postponed to a time when he would be able to consider it properly; so we allowed ourselves to be shown to our rooms without demure. At any rate, I comforted myself, if someone had been shooting at Stuart-Wortley's car in London, it was then unlikely that down here in Hampshire he would be in any danger; and the morning would be early enough to report the matter.

It was sometime after three in the morning when I was awoken by the sound of the engine of a motorcar, then the noise of banging doors, followed closely by the sound of running feet in the passage outside my door. Throwing back the bedclothes I went over to the window and pulling aside the heavy curtain I espied a large shiny black vehicle displaying a gold and red crest upon its bonnet; surely this was not the Hampshire Constabulary come to investigate a heinous crime? But no; the sight of liveried servants buzzing around the motor car like bees around a hive convinced me that this must be the arrival of the guest who's lateness had so upset the Colonel.

I could not imagine who this august personage might be, but bed was calling me and I concluded that the morning would come quite soon enough and with it would also come the nature of their identity.

ONE

The servant bringing me hot water awakened me, and as he pulled back the curtains, he informed me that it was eight o'clock; that it was presently dull and misty; that rain was anticipated before lunchtime; and that breakfast would be in twenty minutes.

I had hardly completed my toilet when Holmes presented himself.

"Good morning, Watson. Did you hear the commotion in the night?"

"Indeed I did," I replied rather peevishly as I attached my watch chain to my waistcoat. "I have no idea who the visitor was, but I rather wish that he had chosen a more appropriate time to arrive."

Breakfast at Highcliffe proved to be an informal affair with guests serving themselves from silver dishes from the breakfast room sideboard and taking such seating as was available. Holmes and I were apparently not the only guests whom had suffered from an interrupted nights sleep; all present had been inconvenienced by the late arrival. Taking my selection from the scrambled eggs, kedgeree, sausages, bacon and kidneys, I squeezed myself between Sir Sidney Chambers the newspaper magnate (who it appeared was breakfasting without his lady wife) and Mr Spencer, the radical Member of Parliament who had dealt himself lavish proportions of everything on offer and was now consuming the fare at an alarming rate.

"Good morning, Doctor Watson," he said, his mouth full of scrambled egg and toast. "Did you get a sight of our late arrival last night?"

I shook my head and admitted I had not.

"Pity," he said spearing some kidneys with his fork. "I'd like to have given the blighter a piece of my mind."

Sir Sidney laid a hand upon my arm and addressed both Spencer and myself.

"Gentlemen; if you please," he looked around the room in a rather conspiratorial fashion; then seeing us to be presently unobserved by the others he addressed us in a hushed voice. "I believe that it was the arrival of our guest of honour which disturbed your slumbers last night."

"Indeed," rumbled the Member of Parliament. "How the devil do you know that?"

"Well; last week when the Colonel served me with his invitation, he told me that there was a very special reason for asking me down, because he desired me to meet an august personage whom it has long been my desire to interview for my newspaper, *The Clarion*. Now there is only one person in the whole world whom my newspaper has regularly supported and wished to promote here as a great friend of our country and it is my belief that it is he who has come to Highcliffe."

The Member of Parliament and I looked at each other blankly, and I shrugged. Then Spencer seemed to catch on.

"You don't mean that **he** is here?" he said sharply.

Sir Stanley nodded.

"I believe so," he replied positively beaming.

I looked from face to face with total incomprehension. "Who is here," I demanded.

The newspaper owner looked at me in some surprise.

"Why, Doctor Watson, clearly you do not take my title, otherwise you would understand. We have here in our midst none other than the Emperor of Imperial Germany, Kaiser Wilhelm."

"The Kaiser!" I cried.

I felt a hand upon my shoulder. It was Sherlock Holmes.

"Watson, my dear fellow, did you not realise?"

I shook my head.

"Ah," he said, "but did you not observe the large Daimler-Benz with the imperial crest emblazoned upon it when you were awakened so early this morning? When I saw it I knew at once that we were to be graced by the presence of the German Emperor."

I stood up from my place and returned to the sideboard to deposit my used plate and pour myself some coffee. Holmes accompanied me.

"Well, thank you, Holmes," I hissed. "You might have informed me earlier and not just left me to make a fool of myself before those two fellows."

He smiled.

"I would not concern yourself, Watson. Already they have forgotten your existence in their mutual excitement."

I snorted.

"A common place psychological condition, Holmes. The fellow who believes himself to be on a social par with his companions will inevitable drop him immediately for another he perceives to be of a higher rank."

Holmes looked thoughtful.

"Then, my dear fellow, it is just as well that I do not move in society where rank is deemed to be superior to friendship, for it is my belief that friends are to be cherished and not dropped when someone more glamorous comes along."

We were interrupted by Colonel Stuart-Wortley, who despite the many calls upon his attention by the other occupants of the breakfast room sought out Holmes and myself; he stood between us with hands resting upon our shoulders and spoke quietly to us.

"Gentlemen, you will by now have discovered the identity of our distinguished guest. His Imperial Majesty is delighted to have you here and has expressed a strong desire to meet you both at your earliest convenience; and as I observe that you have already breakfasted, then there is no time like the present. That is of course, if you are both agreeable?"

TWO

The Kaiser, we were informed had taken up residence in the library which he had apparently decreed that for the rest of his stay was to be his inner sanctum. The Colonel knocked timidly upon the high oak panelled door and we waited for permission to enter; then the door was partially opened and we were presented with the image of a crop-headed middle aged fellow dressed in a blue uniform trimmed with gold.

"Mr Holmes and Doctor Watson to see his Majesty, Maxim" said Stuart-Wortley.

The servant nodded and indicated that Holmes and I should enter, but as the Colonel made to follow us Maxim's hand was placed firmly in the centre of the old soldiers chest stopping him sharply in his tracks.

"I say," he spluttered in evident surprise.

"These people his Imperial Majesty wishes to talk with alone," the servant replied in a voice, which although quiet in it tone, indicted quite securely that his wishes were not to be ignored. Stuart-Wortley shrugged his shoulders and sighed.

"Very well, gentlemen," he said resignedly, "you had

better go in without me."

The door was opened fully as the servant led Holmes and myself into the library. The book-lined room was of immense proportions and was decorated in a Georgian style with beautiful plaster decorations; particularly pleasing, were the ceiling moulds and configurations. There were a number of high windows with a strip of stained glass running across each one and I imagined that upon a sunny morning the light cast through them must have been exceedingly attractive. Beyond lay a wide path by a large expanse of neatly clipped lawn filled with formal box-edged flower beds; and further on, stood a plantation of mature oak trees, now all but denuded by the autumnal chill.

The Kaiser was sitting at a large roll-top desk working on some papers; he was wearing a white uniform resplendent with Military decorations and golden embellishments. The detritus of his breakfast lay strewn over the polished top of what my Irish friends refer to as a *wake table*. Clearly this large furnishing had been purloined from another part of the house for use at the Kaisers' convenience during his stay at Highcliffe; and if it upset the careful harmony of the décor, it mattered little to the occupant, for as he looked up from his papers to speak to his servant, his face bore upon it an expression of calm contentment.

"Your Majesty, here is Herr Holmes and Herr Doctor Watson."

The Kaiser laid down his pen and stood up to greet us revealing that the trousers of his uniform had been designed to resemble jodhpurs; his boots I could see were knee length and shiny black. He dipped his right hand momentarily into the pocket of his tunic as if quickly depositing something he did not wish us to see; then he thrust it out towards Sherlock

Holmes in the time honoured way.

"Mr Holmes, a pleasure," he said in a warm rich voice, grasping my friend firmly by the hand. The two men gazed at each other and Holmes gave a little bow.

"His Imperial Majesty has a fine grip."

A peculiar glint came into the eyes of the Kaiser, then he sharply withdrew his hand and looked at it with a rueful smile.

"Mr Holmes, you were on to me, were you not?"

Holmes laughed and bowed his head slightly.

"As soon as I observed your Majesties hand re-emerge from your pocket I saw that your rings hand been turned inward. I supposed that you were intent upon surprising me."

The Kaiser gazed at Holmes for a moment, his dark eyes stern, then he laughed, the peal of his laughter echoing around the room and literally rattling the glass in the chandelier hanging above his head.

"Mr Holmes, you are a fine fellow indeed!" he cried.

He waved Holmes and myself to chairs before the fire where his manservant served us with coffee.

"Maxim," the Kaiser said, "have my tweeds laid out, and my brogues I think." He collapsed upon the settee and leaned back with closed eyes. "You are surprised that I address my man in English?" he asked suddenly. "You will have a cigarette, yes?" Holmes nodded. The Kaiser reached across to a gold monogrammed box on a small side table and held it open for my friend to help himself, and then he took one himself. The Kaiser took a spill from the holder by the fire and lit it from the flames.

"It is as you say, when in Rome, do as the Romans do." His eyes followed Holmes as he lit his cigarette. Then he continued in a quieter voice. "Although if only one quarter of what my consular official in Rome tells me about the activities of that city's inhabitants is true, then perhaps it would be better if you English changed the adage." Again he laughed uproariously at his jest. "Now, Doctor Watson, you have written eloquently, if I may say, about your adventures with Mr Holmes, perhaps there are one or two you may care to expand upon? I am particularly interested in discovering how things turned out after my fellow monarch, the King of Bohemia, was spurned by the singer Irene Adler. Did she ever bother him again?"

Thus it was for the next hour or so, that Holmes and I regaled the German Emperor with tales of our adventures together and as requested I proceeded to relate how the shadow of Irene Adler had indeed fallen once more across the fate of the unfortunate monarch to which he had alluded. Then there was a re-telling of the dark affair of *Charles Augustus Milverton*, followed by the somewhat humorous matter of *The Red Headed League*, whilst Holmes to finish mentioned the Sussex case he had just written up for publication, and which was the very reason he had been up in London.

It was the return of Maxim that broke the spell, for throughout the review; the Kaiser sat with a dreamy look upon his face clearly enraptured by our narrative. The clattering of crockery and rattle of cutlery as the servant cleared away the breakfast things returned him to the real world. His face broke into a scowl.

"Ach!" he muttered. Then the Kaiser clapped his right hand on his thigh and stood up. "Thank you, gentlemen. It is now time for my morning exercises." He laughed out aloud. "If this was my party I should now have everyone up and taking exercises with me."

The audience clearly being over, Holmes and I made our exit, and then just as my hand was upon the door handle, the Kaiser addressed us one final time.

"Mr Holmes, Doctor Watson; if you please. This is not the Imperial Court; I therefore expect none of the Court routine. You will please observe only the following formalities. When you see me for the first time in the day, you will bow and then, only when you bid me goodnight will you bow again. You should only address me as *sir*. If you observe these simple rules, then my heart will be content. It will also allow the flow of conversation to become somewhat easier. You will obey, yes?"

Colonel Stuart-Wortley was waiting in the corridor for us. Indeed, so close to the egress was he, I literally fell over him. It seemed to me that he had been simply hanging about in the passage for the entire duration of our audience. He smiled broadly at Holmes and myself.

"Well done, gentlemen. When the Kaiser heard about your invitation this weekend, he was extremely desirous of meeting you; and you have performed well for him."

Holmes looked darkly at him.

"Colonel. Doctor Watson and I are not a circus act expected to perform on demand!"

The Colonel coloured.

"No, no, Mr Holmes, you misunderstand me. It is just that when his Majesty is happy, then the sun shines on his friends all day long; and because of you gentlemen, it will shine very brightly today."

I looked sideways at Holmes and sighed.

"I only wish that some folk in my circle would cultivate such an idea."

Holmes laughed and slapped me upon the shoulder.

"But, my dear Watson, you are not the Emperor of Germany and that salient fact precludes such possibilities."

The library door opened once more and Maxim stood there. Stuart-Wortley gazed hopefully at him.

"I believe that it is now your turn, Colonel," said Holmes. He turned to me. "Now, Doctor, let us collect our hats and coats and take a turn in the Colonel's excellent grounds."

THREE

Before long, Holmes and I found ourselves upon the beach of the tiny cove, which skirted the seaward edge of the Colonel's grounds. We descended some steps cut into the cliff-top, then a wooden staircase leading down via a platform to the beach some fifty feet below. The staircase I observed to be relatively new and it afforded a pleasant and easy access to the sea.

Holmes stooped and brushed away a quantity of sand from the base platform and sat down. He signalled to me and invited me to sit beside him.

"Well now, Watson" he said, "What do you make of the Kaiser."

I sighed and blew out my cheeks.

"He is certainly a most engaging personality; and I am much impressed by his determination to remain as informal as his position will allow; but are you asking for a general impression, or are you seeking a detailed analysis of his personality, Holmes?"

Holmes laughed.

"Your pawky humour is showing again, Watson. Now, my dear fellow, I was not expecting a professional opinion of the Kaiser's personality, just merely asking for your general observations."

"Well," I said, "I have observed that he is likely to be of variable temperament; the Colonel's comments show it to be so."

"Some say he is quite mad."

"His enemies, surely?"

"Ah, there's the rub, as Shakespeare says. It is his friends who accuse him thus."

"Abnormal behaviour displays many things but it does not reveal the cause; that may be something as simple as a chemical imbalance, and although this imbalance can cause the sufferer to display erratic behaviour, it does not indicate madness."

"How so?"

"For example, you will recall that George the third was widely supposed to be mad. Well it is just possible that he was suffering from an inherited condition called porphyries, a disease which leads the sufferer to display many of the symptoms associated with clinical madness. Now if the Kaiser does display abnormal behaviour, it is not impossible that as a close family member of our own royal family, he may have inherited the disease. I do not say he suffers from it, I merely put it forward as a possibility."

"Did you notice that his left arm is appreciably shorter than his right?"

"No," I said, "I did not observe."

"Indeed. He tried very hard to ensure that his shorter arm was obscured from our gaze"

"I have seen many photographs of the Kaiser in the

newspaper, but I have never noticed any particular difference."

"Ah, that is because of his particular insistence on holding his gloves in his left hand. This gives an illusion of length."

He took out his pipe and peered into the bowl.

"Now, I believe I have a pouch of tobacco somewhere – Ah!" Very soon he was puffing away contentedly. "Now, Watson; you will have noticed that by contrast his right hand is off great strength." He looked quizzically at his own right hand and flexed it slowly once or twice. "It is a matter to which I may testify fully."

"Quite so," I replied remembering the peculiar handshake that had passed between the two men. "What was that all about, Holmes?"

He laughed.

"That was His Majesties little method of testing the metal of a new acquaintance. It was only when he put his hand into his pocket then withdrew it immediately I realised that his rings were now turned inwards towards the palm of his hand and unless I was able to take swift and remedial action, I would have the sharp facets of his rings digging painfully into the flesh of my hand. So, dear Watson, I prepared my retaliation by striking first. I held his hand in a grip such as even Hercules himself could not break. It was a hold I had discovered many years before when studying baritsu. I imagine that you noted the look of surprise which came over his face when we shook hands?"

"Indeed I did."

"I fancy that his hand will pain him sufficiently for long enough to remember that he cannot play his tricks upon everyone he meets and expect to get away with it."

An interesting idea struck me.

"It is said that His Majesty the King dislikes the Kaiser intensely, and furthermore I heard somewhere that they are not consumed by the ardour of their mutual regard. I wonder if the Kaisers' penchants for fun and games might lie at the root of his antipathy?"

Holmes shook his head

"That we shall never know, dear fellow. But there is one thing we may extrapolate from these antics and that is the fact that the Kaiser suffers from a physical handicap and is shy about exposing this handicap to public scrutiny. He also desires to impress with the undoubted strength in his good arm and has a tendency towards temperamental outbursts. This leads me to believe that he is suffering from a sense of insecurity and self doubt."

"Well, Holmes," I said, "in a short time we have given the Kaiser an honourable inherited disease and the beginnings of a persecution complex. Pity that we cannot ask Doctor Freud his opinion on at least one of these conditions."

He chuckled.

"Then should we ever be fortunate enough to visit Vienna, my dear fellow, I shall consult the good doctor at once."

Our conversation was rudely interrupted by a shout from above. I looked up to see the Kaiser and Colonel Stuart-Wortley wearing heavy overcoats and descending the staircase.

"Mr Holmes, Doctor Watson; we meet again," the Emperor cried as he jumped the final two steps from the platform to the sandy beach below. Then, without even a perfunctory introduction to the subject, he plunged into the matter presently occupying his mind. "Tell me, gentlemen, what do you think of the present relationship between our two great countries?"

I replied with truthfulness that I had not given the matter very much thought; but Sherlock Holmes was somewhat more direct.

"It is a pity, sir, that the politicians in both countries seem determined to make it worse rather than better."

The Kaiser's face lit up.

"My thoughts entirely, Mr Holmes, although I perceive that much of the fault lies with England. It is unfortunate that whilst I am the only force capable of holding back the anti-British sentiments of my subjects, I am cruelly misunderstood and regarded as the enemy!"

The final sentence was delivered at just a little less than a shout. Clearly this was a subject about which he felt very deeply. The by now red-faced Kaiser sat down upon the platform and indicated that we three should join him there.

"Let me give you another example of how my best intentions have been misjudged. During the South African war I dissuaded, and further more I obstructed, the Franco-Russian plan to intervene as well. Yet I am accused of supplying weapons to the rebels, when everyone knows it was your so-called ally, France, who ignored the *entente cordiale* in doing so. You see how I am misrepresented." Again the Kaiser's voice had risen to a shout and I for one was extremely relieved that it was only the sky and sea, which bore witness to his tantrum. I only hoped that the sound of his voice had not carried to the cliff-top, and had not been overheard by the casual passer-by.

FOUR

It was only when luncheon was over that Holmes and I were able to discuss the Kaiser's outburst, and then it was only after we politely declined the Colonel's invitation to an afternoon excursion to Romsey Abbey in the company of the German Emperor. Matters of a more pressing nature were on the mind of Sherlock Holmes, however, and taking this first opportunity, no matter how brief, he put to the Colonel the matter of the attack upon his car.

Holmes produced the flattened bullet once more and dropped it into the palm of the astonished Stuart-Wortley.

"Are you serious, Mr Holmes? This is a round from a high-powered air gun. Who would do such a thing?"

My friend looked at the Colonel with his piercing eyes.

"I am perfectly serious, sir. At present I cannot say who may be at the heart of this matter. All I can tell you is that I have conceived three separate scenarios, but without further data, I refuse to speculate."

"Then surely you will advise me about security at the very least, Mr Holmes?"

Holmes sighed.

"That is the most difficult aspect of the matter, Colonel, if we do not know exactly why the incident occurred, or who was responsible we are hamstrung. All I can advise is that you take the precaution of having extra staff on duty, particularly when you go out, or come back in. Also ensure that when your guests go about in the wide world that they do not stray into the open for too long."

Stuart-Wortley shook his head.

"That is not particularly encouraging, Mr Holmes; but I understand that there is little else which can be done." He rubbed his chin reflectively. "I am debating with myself whether it is safe for His Majesty to remain here and whether should I inform him."

"That, my dear sir, is a matter upon which I cannot advise, I leave it up to your discretion."

"Well, let us hope that the Kaisers' visit to Romsey is without incident," he said standing up and straightening his tie.

After the Kaiser and his party had departed, Holmes found his hat and coat and took a turn in the castle grounds; he declared that as rain was predicted later he would take his exercise now. For a while I watched him walking slowly and poking about the grass with his stick. Then as I felt that it was high time I attended to the plaintive cries of my publisher for a long awaited article, I decided to retire to my room and rough something out on paper.

I had been sitting at my desk for sometime, the fire had been banked up, but the top of the window was open a little to afford a fresh supply of air, when it happened. Suddenly the door opened and of all people Maxim, the Kaiser's manservant, came silently into the room. Clearly he did not notice me, sitting as I was in the high-backed leather chair.

Turning slightly in my seat, I watched the middle-aged German move on stealthy feet across the room to my bed where he proceeded to sift through my personal effects.

Angered by this gross invasion of my privacy, I threw down my notebook and stood up, my chair scraping loudly upon the wooden floor.

"Maxim; what are you doing? I demand an explanation!"

He made a start, followed by a sharp intake of breath, and then he spun upon his heel to face me.

"Herr Doctor. A thousand apologies. I believed that you were out with Herr Holmes."

"Clearly," I said dryly. "But perhaps you would care to explain yourself before your master when he returns."

Maxim stepped towards me and held out his hands.

"Oh, no, Herr Doctor. You do not understand; it was at the request of my master that I came here. You see he likes Herr Holmes and yourself so very much, he wants to give you a little present when you go tomorrow. So knowing you gentlemen have pipes he instructed me to find the type of tobacco you smoke so he can present you with some." He looked at his feet. "I have been already to the room of Herr Holmes." He reached into his inside pocket and retrieved a black notebook with a golden crest emblazoned upon it. With hurried fingers the servant plucked at the pages and a paper wrapper from a packet of *Burns Mixture* fell out and fluttered slowly to the floor. This portion of his story appeared to be true, for I remember Holmes telling me that *Burns Mixture* was a common place, though rather inferior blend, but that it was the best to be had in Sussex. Maxim jumped forward and plucked the wrapper up from the carpet.

"Hmm," I said. "Then if what you are saying is true, Maxim – and I intend to confirm your story – you will do far better if your master was to forget all about such a gift because in recent years Mr Holmes has preferred *Merrimans* and I doubt if there is any of that to be had outside of London."

The servant relaxed a little and allowed himself a differential smile.

"What ever the mixture, His Majesty will have it sent down for him, Herr Doctor; but I beg you, sir, please do not worry my master for my discovery will make him particularly angry. He will believe it to be a slur on his own integrity."

I gave the matter a momentary thought. It seemed probable that the servant was telling the truth. I determined, however, to ask the Colonel, who probably knew the Kaiser better than anyone in the house, his opinion on the truthfulness of the servants' statement.

"Very well, Maxim, you may go and consider the matter closed."

"Thank you, Herr Doctor," he said quietly, bowing to me as he made for the door. As he passed me, he bent over and retrieved my notebook from the floor where I had thrown it. He handed it to me. "Thank you again, sir; you are very understanding."

I sat in my chair before the fire once more, but the interruption had broken my muse entirely and my concentration was gone. I took out my watch. It was almost four o' clock, time in any well-run house for afternoon tea. I would find one of the servants and make my demands; besides Holmes should be back directly too, and being only half convinced by Maxim's story, I desired to seek his council.

FIVE

It was not until a little before supper time that I was at last able to take up the matter of Maxims sudden uninvited visit to my room with Sherlock Holmes. Although the November night was drawing in, he and I were keen to take in a little fresh air, for the atmosphere at Highcliffe was stuffy and airless. The Kaiser apparently liked a hot house and although he was disinclined to forsake his quarters, the rest of the house had to be heated almost to tropical temperatures in case he should take it into his head to join the rest of the Colonel's guests. The German Emperor it seemed had returned from his sojourn to Romsey in the foulest of moods and the household staff were walking on egg shells as a consequence, so there was little sorrow displayed by the others when it was announced that he intended to remain aloof for the rest of the evening.

A walk was of little consequence either to Holmes, or to myself, for we would both walk regularly, if separately on a daily basis; Holmes along his cliff-top and me twice around the square. As we perambulated the grounds, we were hardly

hardly ever in full darkness, for the light from Highcliffe's many windows flooded out. I mentioned to my friend the visit of Maxim and asked if he could draw any conclusions.

"You know, Watson," he said. "It is entirely possible that Maxim was telling the plain unvarnished truth, perhaps the Kaiser is so taken with us, he desires to present us with a small parting gift on the morrow." He laughed "If we run into anyone coming *poste haste* from the German Embassy tonight, then we may establish it to be the exact truth."

Suddenly Holmes stopped and stood quite still.

"Watson," he whispered, "we are being observed." In the dim light, I could see him take his *Vesta* case from his overcoat pocket. "A smoke, my dear fellow?" he asked just a little too loudly for the occasion, though upon reflection it was clearly meant for the benefit of our invigilator. Then Holmes held up his hands as if to light a cigarette, cupping one hand around the other. Suddenly there came a bright flash as all the *Vestas* were lit followed by the flickering light of the burning sticks; and there in an alcove no more than two feet distant, there stood the figure of a small dark man, dressed in outdoor clothes and carrying a broken shot gun over his arm. The little man jumped.

"God almighty, Mr Holmes!" he said in a soft Irish lilt. "You half scared the life out of me." It was Stuart-Wortley's gamekeeper.

"Good evening, Mr Feeney. You should not be spying on us like that," said Holmes.

The Irishman stepped into the light; he looked a little sheepish.

"I'm sorry, sir; but it's the Colonel. He's insisting that the staff scour the grounds for intruders. Not wanting to disturb you, I slipped into the shadows to let you pass unmolested, like, and no harm done."

"Not at all," said Holmes. "You were securely tucked away. I doubt if another would have noticed your presence." He smiled. "Carry on, Feeney."

The gamekeeper touched his cap and melted away into the darkness once more, whilst Holmes and I continued our perambulations.

"How on earth did you spot that fellow so securely tucked away in that corner, Holmes?" I demanded.

He chuckled.

"I did not see him, Watson, I heard him."

"You heard him?"

"Indeed. I am not sure if he has bronchial trouble, or had just been running, but his laboured breathing was clearly audible to me as we passed him by."

I shook my head; I had heard nothing. It was quite remarkable; Holmes and I were both talking as we walked and yet his ears had plucked out the almost inaudible breathing of the hidden gamekeeper. Sherlock Holmes was by now past middle life, although his hearing it had been demonstrated had diminished not one jot.

Immediately before retiring for the night, some of the gentlemen gathered in the green drawing room for a smoke. Simpson, the radical Member of Parliament, was haranguing young Anderson, the Colonel's land agent, on the subject of the Kaiser's attire.

"Did you see how he was dressed this afternoon, Anderson?" he exclaimed. "All tweeds and plus fours; and that hat! It had more feathers in it than half a dozen partridges. A turkey cock is what he resembled, a damn turkey cock!"

Anderson, on the other hand, was less trenchant.

"Oh, come now, Simpson. The fellow is a stranger to our customs and he simply wouldn't know that gentlemen dress like that only for shooting."

"Like that!" thundered the Member of Parliament. "Like that but not in such an outrageous form. Damn me, if those plus fours were any more voluminous they'd be plus fives?" He laughed loudly at his jest and even Anderson who appeared more sympathetic had to smile. "And what about his dinner togs, eh? Looks like he's better prepared to start a war than eat!"

Then Simpson noticed our arrival.

"Ah, Mr Holmes, Doctor Watson, what do you make of the Kaisers' attire? It seems to me that this afternoon he dressed like a fool, and in that outrageous tunic tonight he looked like a cad."

Sherlock Holmes regarded the Member of Parliament with a steely eye, at which point the laugh became frozen upon his lips.

"Well now, Mr Simpson, what do I think?" he said quietly. "I believe the Kaiser to be a unique and fascinating personality. Indeed the only fool and cad I can see is the one presently sitting before me." His final words were delivered almost in a whisper; but the rapier like thrust in which they were uttered made the Member of Parliament go a nasty putty-like colour. Holmes turned upon his heel and made for the exit. "Come, Watson" he said over his shoulder. "Let us depart for bed; the air in here is stale with old prejudices."

SIX

The morning sun shone through my bedroom window and I mused that in spite of the season, it appeared that the southern coast of England was in for another pleasant day. The spell of fine weather was perhaps a little late in the year to be described as an Indian summer, but possibly with the presence of our Imperial visitor it might well be referred to as a German Autumn. I smiled to myself at the notion as I fiddled with my collar stud and wondered what the Kaiser might make of my humorous thoughts?

Then, my meditation was rudely interrupted by a heavy knock upon my door and the urgent voice of Cooper, the butler, at the other side.

"Doctor Watson, are you awake, sir. Colonel Stuart-Wortley requests that you attend his Imperial Majesty immediately."

"Come in, Cooper," I cried. The butler entered and closed the door silently behind him. "Now," I said slipping on my jacket, "what is this all about?"

Cooper looked at his feet abashed, the first occasion upon

which I could recall him showing even the slightest flicker of emotion; for like all well-trained servants, who were quite used to all manner of household dramas being played out in front of them, Cooper had accustomed himself to being both deaf and blind; but on this particular morning, he was definitely perturbed.

"It is His Majesty, sir. There has been an – incident."

"What do you mean an incident?"

Cooper made a little noise in his throat before replying.

"I really cannot say, sir. All I can tell you is that the Kaiser is in a fearful temper and that the Colonel has the household staff on the edge of panic as a result. Mr Holmes has been summoned as well. Please come at once, sir!" The last sentence was delivered in tones more resembling a plea than a request.

I sighed. Clearly I was unlikely to get anything further out of the butler, but if Holmes was also involved, then I supposed it had to be a serious matter and I should attend as requested. I meekly followed him down the grand staircase and into the great hall. Here I discovered the Kaiser to be in full flow, fulminating against the *rascals and villains* who had perpetrated such a dastardly intrigue. Holmes was there too, with Colonel Stuart-Wortley, Anderson and Maxim.

"Ah, there you are, Watson," said the Colonel as he detached himself from the little crowd of servants waiting nervously at the foot of the staircase.

"His Majesty insisted that you be called to witness the events."

I gazed blankly at my host, but before a single word could pass my lips, Holmes took me by the elbow and propelled me away and into an alcove by the door.

"Watson, my boy, a crime has been committed. His

Majesty has been the victim of a burglar, who has made off with three valuable items. A gold cigarette case, a monogrammed notebook and a statute in the form of an eagle."

"Good heavens!" I spluttered. "When did this happen, Holmes?"

"Unfortunately is seems that it occurred late yesterday afternoon when the house was all but empty."

I took in a deep breath and blew out my cheeks.

"Well it does at least eliminate a number of suspects."

"Indeed. We must be grateful for small mercies, therefore."

Stuart-Wortley who had looked more and more flustered as each moment passed came up and grabbed Holmes by the arm, and forcibly propelled him towards the door of the library where the Kaiser claimed his inner sanctum.

"Please, Mr Holmes, the time for talk has passed, action is now what we need. You are famous for your deep analytical powers; please use them now, sir!"

Holmes gently but firmly extracted himself from the Colonel's grip and stood on the threshold of the library, his eyes darting from corner to corner, his face set in the mask of concentration I knew so well.

"Watson," he said over his shoulder, "please ensure that no-one but myself should enter whilst I am conducting my investigation."

The Colonel and the Kaiser looked at each other. Stuart-Wortley's eyes shifty and nervous, the Emperor's probing.

"You will understand, gentlemen, that Mr Holmes requires space in which to work," I explained. "Equally you must understand that the fewer people who are present in the room during the investigation, the less likelihood there may be of contaminating any evidence."

Sherlock Holmes now addressed the Kaiser.

"Sir. If you would please tell me exactly where the missing objects were taken from, I may then begin my inspection of the library."

The Kaiser revealed that the notebook had been left upon the roll-top desk, the cigarette case was lying on the little side table next to the sofa before the fire, and the eagle had stood upon the ornately carved mantle piece. He also explained that whilst the pieces were of little intrinsic value, they all held a sentimental value for him.

Holmes began his inspection; moving quickly, then slowly as the fancy took him. A moment later he was upon his hands and knees by the tall windows.

"Ah," he exclaimed, "this is interesting." He stood once more and inspected the glass door leading to the grounds. "Broken glass, Watson," he muttered. "Hmm – most indicative." Then he was down upon his knees again and crawling back along to the mantle piece. "Fascinating," he said. Holmes stood up again and proceeded to run his hand over the ornate carvings. He reached into his inside pocket and produced his knife and appeared to remove something from the wood before rubbing his hands together in a fashion I had seen him do many times in the past. He had seen all he needed.

"Come, Watson, I believe we now need to inspect the grounds."

Holmes opened the garden door and signalled for me to follow him leaving the Kaiser and Stuart-Wortley to make their own interpretation of the scene. I followed his swiftly disappearing figure stopping only to carefully step over two heaps of glass; one inside the library and the other considerably larger pile on the step outside. I finally caught up with my friend as he reached the trees that skirted the cliff-top.

"Holmes, what did you find embedded in the mantle piece?" I demanded.

He looked casually at me.

"It was nothing to do with the matter presently in hand I can assure you, Watson. It is merely something we shall come to eventually."

Perplexed, I followed him into the copse and was astounded to see him drop to his knees once more. Again he inspected the ground carefully running his fingers through the dead leaves, twigs and other detritus.

"This is getting better and better, my boy," he cried. "Look at this." Holmes held up a paper wrapper that bore the legend *Burns Mixture*.

"Good heavens! It is a tobacco wrapping. Indeed it is the self-same brand as the one you yourself smoke."

Holmes nodded but said nothing. Instead he took out his pocket book and placed the wrapper carefully between two of the pages. Suddenly his eyes lit up and he dropped to the ground once more.

"This is remarkable and much better than I expected," he cried as he scrabbled away at the leaf litter.

"You have found something else?"

"Indeed."

Holmes stood up again and slowly rubbed the debris from his hands, then before I could enquire further about his find, he was off again through the trees and in the direction of the stairway to the beach below.

"Come, Watson," he cried. "This is where I will make my final discovery."

I was completely at a loss as Holmes seemed to be predicting the outcome of an investigation without having all his precious data to hand; or had he found something in the trees which had convinced him of a further find on the beach? Either way it was my fate to merely follow in his stately wake. As I followed I suppose that I was cast in the roll of the common foot-solider who is neither privy to the thoughts of the commanders, nor open to questioning their orders; he merely follows orders and acts blindly until the campaign is over. Then, and only then, does it become clear to him exactly how the overall plan has been formulated?

"Here, Watson, come and see our prize." I found Holmes standing upon the platform at the foot of the staircase and pointing towards a rowing boat pulled up onto the beach well above the high tide mark. He jumped down onto the sand and strode over to the boat, and as I followed him he bent over, reached into the vessel, and moments later produced an old and rather disreputable looking Gladstone. Holmes perched himself upon the boats' prow and opened the bag. "Aha, my dear fellow. Behold the booty." I peered inside and saw to my delight the missing valuables.

"My word, Holmes!" I cried. "This is excellent. You have discovered the loot before it could be spirited away."

Holmes chuckled and shook his head.

"I do not think so, Watson, as you may observe that this boat has been holed."

I walked around the craft and saw that it's ancient and venerable timbers had been pierced by a heavy blow, and one which was of considerable vintage too, if the discolouring of the broken edges was anything to go by.

"Hmm – you are correct, this boat is going nowhere, except perhaps to the bottom of the sea," I said scratching my head.

"So why were the stolen objects deposited here?"

"Why indeed?" said Holmes quietly.

Then from behind me there came a movement, which made me jump. I spun around to discover Feeney standing behind me.

"Doctor Watson," he said, "is something wrong? I saw you and Mr Holmes just now coming down to the beach and when I saw that old rowing boat on the sand, I thought something must be up."

"No, no," I replied. "Mr Holmes and I were following up a clue that is all."

His eyes fell upon the old Gladstone and Holmes smiled.

"All is well, Feeney. Perhaps you could move the boat a few feet up the beach for us."

"Certainly, sir; anything to oblige," said the gamekeeper tipping his hat.

My attention was quite suddenly drawn to a bright flash of light from the cliff-top above.

"It would appear as if we are being observed," I said. "For surely that was the glint of sunlight upon glass? Perhaps it is the thief watching us and cursing his luck that Sherlock Holmes has thwarted him."

"It is the thief, certainly," my friend agreed, "but I have little doubt that he is not so very annoyed by our discovery; indeed he may even be relieved."

I looked sharply at my companion, but his features bore no clues to what was in his mind. Long years of experience had taught me that it would be a waste of time and effort to demand an explanation now, so I resolved to keep my council until such time as Holmes was prepared to reveal his mind.

SEVEN

It was sometime later when a small number of guests and household staff privy to the events were gathered together in the library at the request of Sherlock Holmes. Present with Holmes and myself, were the Kaiser who sat at his roll- top desk, his servant, Maxim, Colonel Stuart-Wortley, Feeney, the gamekeeper, and Cooper, the butler. The Kaiser was first to speak.

"Now, Mr Holmes, as you have called us here together at the scene of the crime, you have either something to report, or better you intend to unmask one of us as the criminal." He smiled at his little joke. It was rewarded by a spate of chuckles from the assembly.

Holmes walked behind the sofa before the fire and ran his hand along its back, his nails catching at the fabric and making a scratching noise. As he did we all turned around from our seated positions to see what he was doing.

"Let me see, sir," he said, "you are expecting either information or a revelation; is that so?"

The Kaiser glared and swept the room with his good arm.

"I would hope that at the least you have something to tell us, Mr Holmes, for I have urgent matters to which I must attend and have no time to waste on meaningless chatter. Where are my treasures?"

Sherlock Holmes smiled sharply.

"Would Your Majesty care to examine the table by your elbow ..."

There to the astonishment of all, except John H. Watson, on the very table at which we were sitting lay the missing articles. Holmes in his theatrical fashion had used a simple diversion to produce the effect he desired.

The Kaiser almost jumped out of his chair.

"Holmes!" he cried. "Then it is true; you are the genius my uncle, the king, says you are. Excellent!"

Stuart-Wortley stood up and clapped his hands together in delight.

"Well done, Mr Holmes; another case solved. In record time I should think."

I saw Feeney and Cooper look at each other, the little gamekeeper smiled and winked at his colleague; and even the usually impassive butler permitted himself a nod of approval. The Kaiser took up his treasures and re-deposited them in the places from which they had been taken.

"Splendid, Mr Holmes. You have returned my treasures, but do you have the thief?"

Holmes gazed at the Emperor.

"Oh, indeed, sir." He felt into his pocket and took out the notebook and extracted the tobacco wrapper. "It was when I found this that I realised at once who the mastermind behind this crime was."

"Then for goodness sake, Holmes, give him a name!" I cried.

"It is none other than Kaiser Wilhelm, the Emperor of Germany."

A sharp intake of breath came from the assembly and all eyes fell upon the accused man. For a moment the Kaiser stood silently, eyes blazing. All present held their collective breath, silent to a man and expecting at any moment the explosive wrath of the Emperor to burst over the room like a tidal wave – yet it did not come; there was indeed an explosion, but rather than one of wrath it was one of mirth and merriment with his laugh ringing out like a cathedral bell.

"Mr Holmes!" he cried his eyes twinkling with amusement. "You have caught me out. I confess that the culprit was I."

I stared blankly at the Kaiser.

"But, sir, I do not understand why you should desire to steal your own valuables?"

But before the Kaiser could answer my question Holmes interrupted.

"I believe I can answer your question, Watson. It was because His Excellency desired to observe the celebrated Sherlock Holmes in action." He turned towards the Kaiser. "Am I right, sir?" he said sharply.

The Emperor nodded.

"You are exactly right, Mr Holmes. When the Colonel informed me that you had returned to London from your self imposed exile, I could not resist the temptation to impose on him to ask you down here for the weekend, so I could meet you and perhaps test you out."

My friend did not look at all pleased by this revelation and was disposed to express his disapproval vigorously.

"Sir, whilst you may regard the world and everyone in it as

your playthings, I have to tell you that Sherlock Holmes for one is no toy to be taken out of the play box when it suits you."

"Be careful, Holmes," I whispered. "Remember to whom you are speaking; this is no petty official who has stood in your way."

He eyed me sharply and shook his head.

"No, Watson, I cannot agree. Were the Emperor merely some petty official, then he might display a better sense of personal decorum." Once more Holmes faced the Kaiser. "You, sir, must not expect to wind me up, then let me go to perform my tricks and dances. It will not do!"

Once again there was a heavy silence in the room and I could see Feeney gaze at Cooper in wonder. The butler had remained impassive throughout, but I could see him making mental notes for later recapitulation in the servants' quarters. Holmes I feared had temporarily lost control of his sense. Then I studied the Kaiser who I saw to be gazing at my friend with strange impassivity. Perhaps he was making up his mind the exact nature of the punishment he would demand for Holmes.

At last the Emperor found his voice.

"So, Mr Holmes, that is how you see me, as a puppet master, pulling the strings and making people dance to my tune; and you do not approve?"

Holmes nodded.

"I have heard tales of fat generals and large sausages dancing in tutus for your delight. I am no marionette and I shall not dance for you."

The Kaiser surveyed the assembly and when his eye fell upon me, I quailed, but to my amazement there was no trace of the deep and terrible anger I was expecting to see, but instead there was a decided twinkle.

"Doctor Watson, what do you think?"

My brain raced.

'Now, Watson' I said to myself. 'Placed upon the spot you might be, but you have to support and defend your friend in this matter'.

"Well, sir," I said, "whilst I would defer from expressing myself in such trenchant terms as Mr Holmes, what he says is essentially true. You are unfairly expecting too much of another human being, who is after all a personality in his own right, and who must surely be entitled to fair and equitable treatment."

Once again the Kaiser threw back his head and laughed, and as before the glass fitments in the ceiling and much of the china in the cabinets literally rattled and shook.

"Doctor Watson, Mr Holmes," he said wiping his eyes. "You impress me greatly. Well done!"

The assembly relaxed visibly and several of those present broke into smiles.

"So, Mr Holmes," said Stuart-Wortley. "Exactly how did you find His Excellency out?"

The Kaiser retook his seat at the desk and invited Holmes to take a chair. Cooper was dispatched to organise tea whilst Feeney was instructed to make a further inspection of the old rowing boat with a view to affecting repairs. Of the servants only Maxim now remained in attendance.

"Now," said Holmes as he retook his seat at the head of the wake table, "from the very moment when I began my search of the floor, it was self-evident to me that this was no ordinary investigation. As Watson has oft reported in his writings in *The Strand Magazine* vital evidence may be obtained from minute particles. On many an occasion I have gleamed what information I have needed from the smallest of trifles; a single hair or fibre; a trace of mud on a window sill; a trace of cigarette ash; a few specks of gravel on a carpet; these are my stock-in-trade. Yet this morning I discovered evidence so abundant, clear, concise and unequivocal I immediately doubted their honest origins.

"The carpet had upon it not the half expected, half hoped for, traces of footprints, it had instead a line of clear straight prints which were clearly defined as if they had been stencilled upon the carpet. There was sand on the rug before the fire, and yet more sand upon the desk where you are presently sitting, Your Excellency; sand I should not add in tiny amounts, but in quantity. At first I gave serious thought to the possibility that the miscreant was a builder who had taken to burglary on his day off; or perhaps the Kaiser had been secretly building sand castles in the house."

There was a general chuckle of amusement from the assembly and the Emperor slapped his right knee and laughed at the image Holmes had placed in our heads.

"When I next inspected the door to the garden," Holmes continued, "something decidedly odd seemed to have happened to the glass in the pain next to the lock and handle. Certainly the glass had been broken and the key turned, but the broken glass was on the step outside and not on the library floor where it should have been. I immediately asked myself what did this mean."

"It meant, my dear fellow, that the glass had been broken from the inside," I interrupted triumphantly. "But I seem to recall that there was another smaller pile of glass on the inside and that there was a tiny hole a little further up in the door."

"So there was," Holmes agreed, "but I would ask that for the moment that I may be allowed to defer the matter and continue with my narrative ..."

I shrugged my shoulders and nodded.

"Excellent. As I surveyed the ground outside, I observed that although the paving was quite dry there was a further footprint exactly like the others in the library. I ran my fingers over the grass and found it to be quite wet and just a little muddy from the rain we had yesterday evening and last night.

"Of course the wetness of the grass also enabled me to clearly observe that quite recently someone had walked upon it. I could see that a line of footprints led up to the copse above the cliff-top and that they had almost been obliterated by the return of the same person."

"Well," objected Stuart-Wortley, "That is not so surprising, Mr Holmes, our burglar would have made such a journey."

"Indeed, but the one set of prints obliterated by the other would have run contrary to the ones we now have, with the superior set of footprints not leading to the house, but away from it."

There was a murmur of approval from the assembly and the Kaiser nodded. Holmes once more produced the tobacco wrapper.

"It was without doubt my own," he said. "The very one secreted from my room yesterday by Maxim."

"Ah, but you cannot be certain, Holmes," I demurred. "It is as you yourself have said a common place mixture."

"It is and I fancy the local Highcliffe tobacconist will sell it, but it is my own wrapper, nevertheless." He held it up for our inspection. "Although there is a perfectly serviceable device with which to open the packet; see here, a strip that one tears? It has always been my habit to slit the wrapper with my knife; here is the cut. So it was plain as day to me, therefore, that there was no common burglar at work here casually dropping his old *Burns Mixture* wrapper, but another quite different agency."

"Just a moment, Holmes," I said remembering there was another find beneath the tree which had excited his attention. "You discovered something else as well, did you not?"

He nodded.

"Quite right, Watson. But as with your question about the glass, I would beg your patience for a moment or two." Holmes looked at me and I could see a glint in his eye, clearly something was brewing here.

"At the time of my discovery," he continued, "I also espied some more footprints and this time the leaf litter nearby had been kicked up. Here more sand was in evidence but it was well trodden into the soil. A trail for me to follow and no mistake. At the top of the staircase to the beach I could see a rowing boat pulled up onto the beach. This was clearly designed to make me investigate further. Then, as you will recall, Watson, we discovered the missing valuables in a black grip." He looked around for the bag and discovered it to be under the occasional table. "Here, sir," he said to the Kaiser as he held it up for him to inspect, "if you would care to look inside you will note that the lining bears a label in German. Clearly our burglar, if not yourself, was working as our agent, sir."

"But how could you know the bag was not one of His Majesties personal luggage, purloined by the burglar to carry away his ill-gotten gains?" Stuart-Wortley demanded.

Holmes actually laughed at the question.

"My dear Colonel, can you really see one so august as the German Emperor allowing such a disreputable object to remain a part of his personal baggage? It was however more likely to be in the possession of his personal servant, Maxim."

"Then the self same argument could still apply, sir."

Holmes sighed.

"Is it likely that His Majesties servant would be allowed to leave his personal belongings cluttering up the place? Would you allow your man to leave an old Gladstone in the library when he has his own quarters? I think not." The Colonel did not reply, but his expression spoke volumes.

"Upon our return to the staircase, Watson pointed out that we were observed and opined that someone was viewing us through a glass." Holmes jumped up from his seat and strode over to the fireplace. "And here it is," he said triumphantly as he held a large brass telescope aloft. "Was it Maxim or yourself, sir, who was watching our enterprises?"

"It was Maxim," said the Kaiser. "I sent him along the footpath to see how well you were following the trail we had set out for you."

"Indeed," said Holmes, "I suspected as much when I noticed that the boots of your man were quite wet."

The Kaiser burst into a merry laugh.

"Mr Holmes I salute you! Now let me tell you something; I have decided to present you and Doctor Watson with a small gift each as a memento of this weekend. After luncheon I shall telephone the German legation and they will have someone down by nightfall."

If Holmes was grateful for the praise and the promise of a reward, he did not show it, instead he revealed to the Kaiser that his investigation was as yet far from complete. I looked rather darkly at my friend.

"Holmes you have uncovered the matter of the burglary, yet you hint at something else. Will you give it a name?"

Holmes sighed and looked up at the ornate ceiling.

"A name you say, Watson. Very well, let us call it, assassination."

"What!" roared Colonel Stuart-Wortley. "In my house? Mr Holmes; tell me you are joking?"

"Murder is no joke, Colonel."

"Then who is the – target of this assassination?"

Holmes sighed again.

"I am sorry, Colonel, although the evidence is slight, I cannot rule out the possibility that it may be His Majesty."

The Kaiser twitched violently, all trace of humour vanished from his face to be replaced by a look of intense annoyance. He waved his good hand at Holmes as if trying to push away the idea.

"No, Mr Holmes, not here in England."

Again Holmes felt into a pocket and on this occasion produced his pocket-handkerchief. He placed it upon the table before us.

"Here, sir, is evidence; there are no sets of clues placed by Maxim for me to find, no sand from the beach, no carefully deposited footprints, no Gladstone bag, what you will see displayed before you," here he unfolded the handkerchief to reveal it's contents, "are two flattened soft-nosed bullets; one taken from the fabric of the roof of the Colonel's motorcar on Friday, and the other is the one I prised from the mantle this morning." He held up a small shiny brass object. It was clearly the find he had made earlier in the leaf mould. "This is a spent bullet case. It was fired from a high-powered air gun. Behold the small hole in the glass of the door to the garden and the tiny heap of broken glass upon the floor; there is the entry hole."

Stuart-Wortley looked astounded.

"When do you suppose this dreadful incident took place, Holmes?"

Holmes looked at Maxim.

"Do you recall seeing another hole when you broke the glass this morning?"

The servant shook his head.

"No, sir. I am sure that the only one was mine."

"Then it has occurred within the last three or four hours, Colonel."

The Kaiser who had risen from his seat to inspect the door returned to his chair and sat down heavily.

"This fellow must be a cool customer, no?" he said, rubbing his brow.

Holmes nodded.

"Did you see or hear anything, sir?"

The Emperor rubbed his chin reflectively for a moment, then his eyes lit up.

"Yes, Mr Holmes, now you come to mention it, something did happen. It was when I sent Maxim out to lay the clues for you. I watched him for a while as he jumped about under the trees. It was only when he disappeared from view, I gave the matter up. It was as I turned to walk over to my desk that I stumbled rather clumsily over the rug. I heard a tinkling of glass, but as I had bumped into the cabinet, I assumed that in my carelessness I had upset something. I meant to order Maxim to investigate it when he returned, but as yet I have failed to do so."

Holmes jumped up from his chair and quickly peered at the contents of the cabinet, but he found everything to be in order. He smiled his sharply.

"Then, sir, we must conclude that but for your slight accident with the rug, you could by now either be injured, or worse, a dead man."

There was silence in the room. The prospect of the untimely death of a European monarch at the hands of an unknown assassin was something hard to countenance. It would have been not only a terrible disaster, but it also could have led to conflict between England and Germany. And yet the Kaiser seemed to be barely concerned, indeed he actually smiled.

"Well, I have been the object of the assassins bullet in Germany," he admitted. "But they are cowards, afraid for their own skins, who run away when their attempts fails. This fellow will be no different." He looked at Holmes as if seeking confirmation. "At any rate it will not curtail my stay here at Highcliffe. Indeed I have decided, if Stuart-Wortley is amenable, that I will stay for three more weeks." Then for a moment the Kaisers eyes blazed with anger. "No filthy little renegade swine will stop the Emperor of Germany from pursuing his activities!" Again the crystal fittings rattled at the voice of the Kaiser; then just as suddenly as it had arrived his anger disappeared and the look of serenity returned to his face. "So, my friends, let us have no more talk of assassins and continue to enjoy our week-end."

EPILOGUE

The next morning Holmes and I found ourselves in the company of the Kaiser for the final time. True to his word he had gone off earlier to worship at the church of St Marks, Highcliffe quite as if nothing had happened. As Holmes and I were to return to London by the afternoon train, the Kaiser had decided to grant us one last audience. It began in the most informal of ways, for Holmes had convinced me to take the air even though the weather had finally returned to its normal patter. As the footman helped me on with my overcoat, the door to the library opened and the Kaiser steeped out. Just as before, he was dressed in the attire lampooned so cruelly by Stanley Simpson.

"Gentlemen. I am glad to have caught up with you," he said holding out his hand. "I will not see you again before you leave this afternoon, so this is goodbye."

Suspiciously I gripped his hand, half expecting my fingers to be mangled by the Kaisers rings; but no, it was merely a firm friendly handshake.

"Now, Mr Holmes, Doctor Watson, before you depart I have the small gifts I promised you." He waved my friend and I into his inner sanctum and I was surprised to discover that he was not alone; a tall young man stood warming himself before the fire. "Gentlemen let me introduce you to one of Germany's most promising sons. This is Emile Von Bork. I have great hopes for his future."

The young man clicked his heels together in the old and time honoured Prussian fashion and bowed.

"Mr Holmes, Doctor Watson, a pleasure I'm sure."

The Kaiser snapped his fingers and Maxim came forward with two wrapped packages and handed them to his master.

"Gentlemen, these are for you. Please wait until you have returned to London before opening them. Now, Von Bork and I have matters of State to discuss, so, Mr Holmes, Doctor Watson, thank you for all you have done and in future, I shall endeavour to treat my fellow human beings better. Farewell."

Indeed that was the last we were to see of the Kaiser before we left for London. The day had grown old and the weather, so clement in Highcliffe, had now turned unsettled and more autumnal. As I gazed out of the window of our railway carriage at the dark, gloomy landscape, so swiftly passing us by, I heard Holmes make an exclamation of surprise. I turned to look at him with a quizzical eye.

"My dear fellow, what is the matter?"

He held up the little package given to him earlier by the Kaiser.

"Look at this, Watson, it is a pound jar of *Merriman's*."

I laughed.

"Then it is likely that he has given me the same gift. Such is the power of Emperors, eh, Holmes? It allows them to get anything they wish."

Holmes nodded; then suddenly, I was aware of him observing me with an intense expression.

"That is so, Doctor, but I fear a time is coming when such terrible events will overwhelm us all, that all the King's, or Emperor's, horses and men will be unable to put Europe together again."

"Then you believe that war is inevitable, Holmes?"

"Indeed. Brother Mycroft informs me that trouble is unquestionably brewing in the Balkans, where Serbia is at odds with Austria over the question of Bosnia-Herzegovina and conflict appears to be inevitable. If so, then Russia and Germany will certainly feel obliged to intervene on either side."

"And what of Britain and France?" I said. "Indeed, does the apparent number of assassination attempts on the life of the Kaiser have any bearing upon the international state of affairs?"

He pulled a face.

"Britain and France have treaty obligations towards Russia and may yet become embroiled in any conflict. As for the Kaiser, his enemies believe that for as long as he lives, war is all but inevitable."

"Then what is to be done?"

Holmes shook his head.

"I do not know, Watson. All I do know is that slowly, but surely, Europe is inching towards war."

For a long time, silence reigned in the railway carriage and only the clatter and rumble of the wheels were to be heard. Then I unwrapped the gift, given so kindly to me by the Kaiser. It also contained *Merriman's*. I smiled weakly as I exhibited it to Holmes.

"I hope most sincerely that I shall be spared sufficient time to enjoy its contents."

Holmes chuckled and nodded. He was clearly of a like

mind, for he reached for his pipe and proceeded to help himself from his own jar; and very quickly, his head became wreathed in aromatic smoke. Once again, silence reigned whilst we enjoyed the Kaiser's gifts. Then Holmes smiled.

"We shall be in London soon, Watson; and as I judge that death and destruction is some little way off, we may cheer ourselves up tonight by taking a table at Marcinis. What do you say, old fellow?"

I nodded and smiled back at my friend.

"An excellent suggestion. Holmes; an excellent suggestion."

Sherlock Holmes will return
in a new adventure

Sherlock Holmes

at the

Raffles Hotel

by

John Hall

"With five volumes you could fill that gap on that second shelf"
(Sherlock Holmes, *The Empty House*)

So why not collect all 38 murder mysteries from Breese Books at just £7.50 each? Available from all good book stores, or direct from the publisher with free UK postage & packing. Alternatively you can get full details of all our publications, including our range of audio books, and order on-line where you can also join our mailing list and see our latest special offers.

Baker Street Studios Limited, Endeavour House, 170 Woodland Road,
Sawston, Cambridge CB22 3DX
www.baker-street-studios.com, sales@baker-street-studios.com